LOVE and TENNIS
By Alfred Slote

MACMILLAN PUBLISHING CO., INC. / New York

Macmillan Publishing Co., Inc.
866 Third Avenue, New York, N.Y. 10022
Collier Macmillan Canada, Ltd.

Printed in the United States of America

10   9   8   7   6   5   4   3   2   1

LIBRARY OF CONGRESS CATALOGING IN PUBLICATION DATA

Slote, Alfred
   Love and tennis.

   SUMMARY: A 15-year-old tennis player's experiences in
the world of competitive sports help him come to terms
with his parents' divorce, his first romance, and his own
ambition.
   [1. Tennis—Fiction.   2. Divorce—Fiction]   I. Title.
PZ7.S635Lo   [Fic]   79-14914   ISBN 0–02–785870–7

FOR BOB AMUSSEN

"Remember, tennis begins with love."

—sign in the locker room of the
Arborville Racquet Club, Arborville,
Michigan

I. Arborville

ONE Later, a lot of people told me they knew all along I was going to upset Rob Parker in the quarterfinals that day, but it certainly didn't look that way at the start. When Rob got his first service in to begin the match, instead of just getting it back in play, I slammed it furiously against the fence behind which Matt Bigby and my mother were sitting.

Matt had arrived during the warm-ups and had sat down next to my mother just as though he owned her. And then he started calling out to me in that big voice of his: "Go get'm, kid," as though he owned me.

I tried to concentrate on Rob, but it was hard. My mother was sitting there, watching me closely, and Matt was leaning over, talking to her . . . and to me.

Rob's serve shot by me. An ace that wasn't an ace. I just hadn't moved.

The silence from the hundred or so spectators was deafening. They must be wondering if a fifteen-year-old kid belonged in the quarterfinals of the Arborville Men's Open.

"C'mon, Buddy," Matt shouted, "wake up, boy."

Did he think he was at a football game? I walked angrily along the base line to the forehand court.

"You OK, Buddy?" Rob called out.

"I'm fine," I snapped.

Someone in the stands snickered.

Rob bounced a ball, getting ready to serve again. He didn't have a big serve. It didn't kick as high as Dad's, it wasn't as tricky as Mr. Hankins's, but Rob could put it where he wanted to. He used his first service, not to win points, but to set up the next point.

He served a high kicker to my forehand. I caught it rising and top-spun it back cross-court. He sliced to my backhand. Steady-eddie at his task. I hit a hard drive to his forehand.

He smacked it down my forehand line. I was running. I got to it and sent it down the line. He hit a beautiful little backhand drop shot. I just watched it. There was applause. For both of us, really. I hadn't blown the point. Maybe, they must be thinking, I'd make a match of it.

And then Matt shouted: "That's the way, Buddy."

I netted my return of service for the fourth and last point of the game. He has got to shut up, I thought angrily. Why doesn't she shut him up? No one invited him here. No one wants him here.

I was rattled. I knew I was rattled. But there was nothing I could do about it. As I walked to the bench I looked up in the stands where Chris was sitting. Chris made a little fist at me. Get tough, she was saying. Cut it out. Stop it. Chris thought I had a chance to beat Rob Parker. Chris and my mother did.

Chris was sitting next to her mother, Carol. Carol smiled at me. Dad should have been there by now, if he was coming at all. I guessed he was busy.

I sat down. Rob was into his Gatorade already. I toweled off. Not that I'd worked up a sweat, but it's a good idea to get a changing-sides rhythm.

I waited for Rob to start psyching me again, but now that the match had actually started, he was silent. He knew I was stewing about something. Best to let me stew. Before the match, he had been all psych though.

"You been wiping out the big shots, huh, Buddy?"

Or: "You're about six feet tall now, aren't you?"

Or: "What did you ever do to Tom Stolle? Six–four; six–three. Wow."

"Cut it out, Rob." I was embarrassed that he even thought it was necessary to lay a psych job on me.

In all the years we had played together, I had never won a

single set off Rob. He was eighteen; I was fifteen. He was Class A high-school singles champ of Michigan, on his way to Rollins on a tennis ride. I was playing in my first men's open. I'd won the sixteen-and-unders, but that's a kids' tournament.

In the men's open my first three matches had been against weekend players, but then in the fourth round I ran into Mr. Stolle, who was seeded third and used to play for Harvard years ago. The seeds this year went like this:

> 1st SEED: Ed Hankins (he won last year)
> 2nd SEED: Dr. Richard Berger (my dad, he won the year before)
> 3rd SEED: Tom Stolle (ex-Harvard)
> 4th SEED: Jerry Stoner (ex-Michigan varsity player)
> 5th SEED: Rob Parker (everyone was picking him to win in an upset, since he was beating everyone in practice matches)

There were five more seeds, but they didn't really count. I was unseeded and didn't count in anyone's eyes except my mother's. It was her idea that I should enter the men's.

"You're ready for it, Buddy."

"I'll get creamed."

"No, you won't. You may lose, but no one in this town is going to cream you. You may even be ready to take your father."

I laughed. (I didn't understand it all then.) I said: "The day hasn't come when I'll beat Dad."

She didn't say anything. My mother was always cool. It was what made her such a great tennis player. She never let you know what she was thinking. But the next day she registered me for the men's open. And now I was in the quarter-

7

finals. I had beaten Mr. Stolle because he was relaxed playing a fifteen-year-old and I hit harder than he expected, and
he just never could get his game going. But Rob had
watched our match. (He was scouting Mr. Stolle.) And there
would be no surprising Rob. Rob was no weekend player.

Applause greeted Rob as he walked to his side of the
court. Almost like the big time, I thought, picking up my
racket. Except there were no ball boys or linesmen. You
made your own calls till the finals. The city provided an
umpire for the finals.

There were some scattered handclaps as I walked to my
side. I thought I could hear Chris's hands among them. She's
my girl. She'd root for me no matter what happened.

As I walked to the base line I tried not to look at Mom and
Matt, but it was hard because I was walking toward them. I
wouldn't be facing them when I played, but I was only a few
feet away from where they sat behind the fence. Mom
always watched matches from there, in a lawn chair under
the pine trees.

They were both watching me. I tapped the balls up and
turned my back to them.

"All set, Buddy," Rob called out. His way of letting me
know I was keeping him waiting.

I tossed the ball up. I have a big serve. It's my big offensive weapon . . . against kids anyway. I blasted the first one
. . . out by inches.

Matt whistled. I netted the second one.

"C'mon, Buddy," a different male voice called out, "bang
away."

It was my coach, Mike Higgins. I hadn't seen him before
the match. He must have just gotten there. Mike's the coach
of the university tennis team and owns an interest in the
indoor club. He's a good guy and a great coach.

8

"Play your game, Buddy."

I nodded. It was what Dad would have said. Don't let up.

Rob sent a ball back to me and I got ready to serve to his backhand court. I tried for an ace down the middle. It just missed. Fair call. I hit my second service to his backhand. He sliced it back. Short strokes. Steady, always playing within himself. Let me make the errors.

I slammed his slice cross-court. He anticipated well. He was fast. He caught my ball rising and undercut it to my backhand. I got to it and hit through the ball well, hitting it cross-court. You can really hit well like that when you're running.

The problem was, I wasn't quick. And I couldn't get back in time. Rob anticipates so well. He just sliced my return down the backhand line, within two inches of the line, and I was nowhere near it. He was a sharpshooter. And I was a pigeon.

"Good shot, Rob," I said.

Applause. Relief in the applause. Tennis players (that's who the spectators were) like good rallies.

I was down, love–thirty, but feeling better. The racket wasn't yet a part of my arm, but it was getting there. The outside world was beginning to fade. I'd try to blast a hard first service in there and come up to the net on it.

"You're getting to him, Buddy," Matt Bigby said.

I almost turned when he spoke. Why didn't she stop him? She had to know. I paused. And then I heard her say: "Matt, you're upsetting his concentration."

I banged my first service in and came up to the net after it. Rob timed it beautifully and blew it right by me. Bang, bang. I was helpless. If he did that to my best serves. . . .

Applause.

Now what? I looked over to the sidelines for help. Mike

9

Higgins nodded to me, telling me not to worry, to keep hitting hard. Chris was frowning. Carol, who wasn't a tennis player, smiled at me. She didn't realize Rob had just crucified my best serve.

Love–forty. Spot it in the corner, I thought. I missed the corner. Rob moved in for the second serve. I hit it hard . . . and out. Second love game in a row. And again a deafening silence.

I hit the third ball over to Rob and looked at my racket. If only the answers were in my racket. My eyes met Mom's. She was trying to tell me something. But I wasn't getting the message.

"Set, Buddy?" Rob called out.

"Yeah."

But I wasn't. How was I going to beat this guy? Or even just give him a workout?

He sent a top-spin over. I hit it back hard and he sliced deep to the base line and it was run, run, run. I got one point in the third game when I caught the base line on a shot he (and I) were sure would be out.

Love–three. I sat down on the bench and reached for the mixture of orange juice and tea that Mom made for me. And for herself, for her own matches.

I looked up. She was standing over me. I looked past her to where they had been sitting.

"Matt's gone, Buddy." She crouched down in front of me. "Buddy, you're not going to beat him playing your game. You've got to change up on him. Take something off the ball. Start dinking and slicing. Bother his rhythm. Let *him* make errors."

I stared at her. She really shouldn't be here. The players' bench is the players' bench. You don't coach on the players' bench. And then what was she saying? Telling me to play a junk game. I wasn't a junk player. She knew that. Dad had taught me to be a pure hitter. A form hitter. To hit out all the time.

Mike Higgins, my coach, said the same things. "You'll be ranked some day, Buddy, if you keep on hitting. It's speed and power that will get you to the top."

Now she was telling me to throw up junk.

I shook my head.

"Buddy," she said, pulling the towel away from my face so she could see into my eyes, "you want to win, don't you?"

"Sure."

"Then junk him. Drop shots. Lobs. Slices, spins. Then hit a drive. Do it for me, Buddy. I want you to win this."

"What do you say, Buddy?" Rob called out. He was waiting for me. I hadn't even seen him go by.

I stood up. "I'm OK, Mom."

"Do it, Buddy," she whispered urgently.

Then she walked back to her lawn chair under the pine trees. If I was rattled before, I was plenty rattled now. How did you change everything you were taught to do? Starting with my serve now. I have a good, hard, flat serve. True, Rob was laying back. Still. . . .

If Dad were here, I could take a cue from him. . . .

Mom looked at me.

OK, OK, I thought. I will.

Rob swayed from side to side, four feet behind the base line, waiting for my power.

I dinked my first serve in. Like a little kid. It dropped just over the net.

Rob was in in a flash. He wristed a return. But it wasn't hard, and he was at the net for the first time. I hit a good top-spin lob over his head for a point. My first point!

There was applause. Not for the serve but for the top-spin lob. Rob saluted the shot with his racket.

He was still playing deep for my serve to his backhand

11

court. I laid another dink in there. I could hear sounds of surprise go up from the spectators.

Rob hustled in, and God knows what made me do what I did next. But I came running in too, daring him, challenging him, disconcerting him. He wristed it right at me. I stepped aside and slammed a hard forehand right back at his feet. He couldn't handle it.

Again applause. He stared at me and then shook his head. I'd won two points now. But it wasn't tennis, what I'd just done. Charging in recklessly like that. The clapping went on awhile. Mom didn't clap though. She never clapped. She expected me to win.

After that things started to go better. I dinked, Rob came in, I hit hard, lobbed. I was working to disturb his head and his game. I pattycaked, drop-shot, sliced, and after a while he began getting exasperated and making errors.

Soon it was 2–3 and a ball game again. Chris stood and clapped as we sat down before the court change. Mike Higgins looked grave. I knew he didn't like me to play this kind of game. Well, Mike, I thought, if I played my game I'd be losing.

Rob won his next service to make it 4–2 but it was a tough game. Then I won mine to make it 3–4. Then it was a big game. I pattycaked, sliced, stalled, ran and got him to make a few crucial errors. He lost his service for the first time that day and the score was 4–4.

After that he was finished, and we both knew it. Something had passed between us. A kind of power. He missed an easy overhead, the kind I used to miss till one day Dad took me out on these same old courts at Sampson Park and showed me how not to clutch on overheads, how to relax by deciding *where* I wanted to hit them, and not wonder *if* I was going to hit them.

12

I went ahead, 5–4. Rob was worried now. His short strokes got even shorter. He tightened up. He double-faulted twice into the net and I took the first set after having been behind love–three.

It was more of the same in the second set, though I was hitting less junk and more power. I aced him to start the set. Rob fought back, he ran, he worked, but just when he'd start grooving on my power, I'd hit a few dopey dink shots to get him thinking again. He went off his game completely, and to the astonishment of every tennis player in Arborville, Michigan, I beat Rob Parker in the quarterfinals. Though, as I said before, a lot of them said they knew I was going to do it all along.

My last shot hit the tape and rolled over. A junk shot with lady luck riding on it.

I ran up to the net to shake his hand. "I'm sorry, Rob," I said, trying not to grin.

"The hell you are," he growled, and then forced a smile onto his face. People were clapping loudly. But I could hear him dying inside.

"Do me one favor, Buddy."

"Sure."

"Win the whole thing, huh?"

Chris came running down from the stands to hug me. I wanted to kiss her, but I knew Mom was watching.

Mike Higgins shook my hand. "Not how I would have done it, lad, but well done."

"Thanks, Mike."

The juniors were all over me then. Paul Cotter, Joel Cohen, both good friends.

"Way to go, Hamburger," Paul said. "But where'd you learn that slop from?"

"From you." I laughed, relaxing finally, one arm around

13

Chris. I'd just beat Rob Parker. The best eighteen-year-old player in Michigan, ranked in the Midwest too. I'd have to pinch myself later.

"That wasn't slop," Chris said, defending me. "He was mixing his shots up."

"Rob's really pissed, isn't he?" Joel asked.

"I guess."

"Hey," Cotter said, "here comes Lamson for the big interview. You're gonna have your name all over tomorrow's paper, Hamburger."

"I hope so," Chris said.

Ann Lamson was the tennis reporter for the *Arborville News* and a good player herself. She once won a match from Mom.

"Congratulations, Buddy. It was simply fabulous how you stole that match from him."

I winced.

"He didn't steal it," Chris said, "he won it."

Ann laughed. She got her pencil and pad out. "What made you change your game when you were down love–three?"

"Being down love–three," Chris said.

Everyone laughed. "What do *you* say, Buddy?" Ann asked.

The honest answer was that my mother made me change my game plan. But I couldn't say that. I just said: "I had to do something, Ann. He was killing me. I was lucky. Real lucky. I've never beaten Rob before. I—"

"Nothing lucky about that top-spin lob," Joel said.

"Hey, you know something," Cotter said, "we might have a Berger–Berger final. Buddy's in the semis now. And if he gets by Mr. Hankins—"

"Which I won't."

They ignored me. It was dawning on all of them, and now on me too, I guess. . . .

14

"—and if Dr. Berger beats Jerry Stoner, which he always does . . . then it'll be son against father." Cotter whistled. "That ever happen in this tournament before, Ann?"

"I don't know. I'll have to look it up. It would be a good lead though."

Her pencil moved quickly over the pad. Everyone began talking about that. Other kids came up to congratulate me and pound my back. I kept telling everyone I was lucky. I felt Chris tug at my arm.

"Buddy, Mom wants to congratulate you too."

"Sure."

We broke out of the excitement and went over to Carol. Looking back on it, that was a mistake. My mother was waiting too. I noticed Matt Bigby hadn't come back yet. I should have gone over to her first and thanked her. She was the real winner today.

TWO "I'm sorry your father wasn't here today, Buddy," Carol said. "I know how pleased he's going to be."

"Where is he?"

"They scheduled him into the operating room at noon. But I'm going home right now and call him. He'll want a blow-by-blow report of the match."

"From Buddy, not us," Chris said.

Carol smiled. "Do you think you could have dinner with us tonight, Buddy?"

I started to say "sure" because I wanted to say it. But instead I said: "I don't know."

"Ask her," Chris said. "She's got to be happy with how you played. Tell her it's only a picnic in the yard and there are other people coming," Chris said.

15

Carol and I looked at her in surprise. Chris never lied. She never schemed. But right now she looked back at us defiantly, and we both laughed.

"Say nothing of the sort," Carol said. "Just ask her. And I do think you ought to go over there right now and talk to her about the match."

"Why doesn't she come over here like everyone else does and congratulate him?"

"Chris," Carol warned.

Chris understood absolutely nothing about my mother. Mom was queen of the Arborville tennis scene. She never went up to anyone. People came to her. At matches she sat in her old raincoat on a lawn chair and people paid homage to her. She was the best woman player in town. She had been for years. She wouldn't come over to congratulate me or anyone. I should have gone right over to her after shaking hands with Rob.

"Go share this victory with your mother, Buddy," Carol said.

"Don't forget to ask her about dinner," said Chris.

"I won't, but don't count on it."

"Ask nicely!"

Carol and I laughed. I picked up my rackets, shook hands with a dozen more people, reported my score to Paul Donaldson, who ran the tournament, and then made my way to where Mom was sitting.

I didn't think she'd let me have dinner with Dad, Carol, and Chris no matter how well I'd played. She hated Carol, which was natural enough. She disliked Chris, which was understandable. And, of course, she was still bitter about Dad. I never talked about my visits to their home.

Ruth Brady, an old friend of Mom's, was sitting where Matt had been. I didn't much like Mrs. Brady. She had said

16

a lot of mean things about Dad when he and Mom split up. She had been kind to Mom, I guess, but I just didn't trust her. When people get divorced, everyone takes sides except the kids.

"Well," Mrs. Brady said in that amused tone of hers, "the conquering hero has finally made it through his hordes of admirers to his mother."

I didn't say anything.

Mom just looked at me. Her face was tanned and taut, as it always was, but her eyes were not angry. "He deserves it, Ruth. He played well."

Compliments from my mother on my tennis game were rare.

"Thanks, Mom."

"Sit down, Buddy."

Mrs. Brady stood up. "I'm going to catch the women's doubles. Joan Ogilvie is supposed to be playing well."

"I'll be right with you, Ruth."

"Congratulations from me too, Buddy," Mrs. Brady finally said. "You did play well."

"Thanks a lot, Mrs. Brady."

"You have a wise tennis head on your shoulders. I know you'll beat Ed Hankins and you'll give your father a good drubbing too."

I didn't say anything to that. There was too much emotion in her words.

Mom said: "Sit down, Buddy."

"Mom, I was wondering if tonight I—"

"Sit down, Buddy."

I sat down.

"That was the best tennis I've ever seen you play."

It was freaky tennis, I thought.

"You played to win."

17

"Your advice helped."

"We had to do something. You were off to a terrible start."

That, I thought, wasn't all my fault. "Can I ask something?"

"Of course."

"Is Matt going to come to all the matches?"

"He feels very involved in your success, Buddy."

"Why?"

"He just does." She looked flustered for a second. She didn't often look flustered.

"If he comes, can he at least be quiet?"

"I'll try, Buddy. He's like a big St. Bernard." She smiled. "He has to bark."

I was going to say that dogs don't belong at tennis matches, but for once I had the sense to shut up.

"As a matter of fact I asked him to come today, Buddy, because he's doing a special favor for us. The reason he left was to make an important phone call for you."

"For me?"

"I'll explain in a minute. He's coming back now. Buddy, I want you to be nice to him."

"Why?"

"Because I'm asking you to."

"I don't like him."

"But I do."

"Mom, he's about the worst—"

I stopped. Matt's voice boomed out: "Hey, I hear I missed the match of the year. Congratulations, kid. I knew you'd get the bum in the end."

I winced. Mom smiled. "Easy, Matt. They can hear you all over."

"Hell's bells, it's the truth, isn't it? Congrats, Buddy."

He held out his hand.

"Thanks," I said and tried to squeeze his hand back in self-defense, but his grip was too strong. He had been a star high-school football player a long time ago. Now he owned a big construction company. Everything about Matt Bigby was big . . . and painful.

"Did you get in touch with him, Matt?"

"I did. Everything's set. He's coming!"

"Matt, you're wonderful." Her voice was like a girl's.

"I've been trying to tell you that for years."

I stood up. I hadn't the slightest idea what they were talking about, but I was sure it had nothing to do with me.

"Mom, can I eat over at Chris's house tonight?"

Matt laughed. "Buddy, I don't think you'll be wanting to eat there tonight."

"Why not?" I tried to keep my temper. Who was he to tell me where I'd be wanting or not wanting to eat?

"Can I tell him, Helen?"

"Of course."

"Buddy, you've heard of Hans Steger, haven't you?"

Dumb question. Who hadn't heard of Hans Steger? He was one of the most famous tennis coaches in America. He ran Tennis World down in Florida. And guys like Connors, Tanner, Stockton, Gerulaitis, you name it—they'd all been pupils of Steger's at Tennis World at one time or another.

"What about him?" I asked, cautiously. I was getting small but bad vibrations.

"Your mother found out that he was in Chicago for a rules meeting of the USTA and she got the bright idea of me giving him a call and asking him to stop by Arborville on his way back to Florida. He said to call back today and he'd let us know. So I called back, and you know what convinced him?"

"What?" Mom asked.

19

Matt grinned. "I told the old man that Buddy was beating the pants off Rob Parker, a ranked player."

"But I wasn't when you left."

"I knew you wouldn't make a liar out of me," Matt said, laughing.

Mom laughed too. I didn't laugh. It wasn't funny. He had no right to do things like that.

"He's coming in, kid. On the Amtrak, at seven-thirty."

My stomach did a flip-flop. I didn't want to meet Hans Steger. I'd had enough of tennis for one day. I'd won my match, why couldn't they leave me alone?

"The number one tennis coach in the world wants to take a look at the hottest fifteen-year-old player around. How about that, sports fans?" Matt let out one of his patented belly laughs. "I've made reservations for the four of us at the Stationhouse for seven P.M." Another roar of laughter. "Just in case the train is early." And then to me: "That's why you don't want to eat at your girl friend's house tonight."

"I want you to dress up, Buddy," Mom said. "We'll leave for the restaurant at six-thirty. Matt, you've done wonders."

"Nothing at all, ma'am."

"Why do I have to dress up?"

"Because I want you to make a good impression on Mr. Steger."

"Why?"

"Tennis World is a very tough place to get into, kid," Matt said.

I stared at him. And then at Mom. I could feel the noose tightening.

"Who said I wanted to go there?"

Mom flashed Matt a warning look, but he plunged in anyway. "Kid, you're good, but you're not that good. You can learn something down there."

"I want you to wear a jacket and a tie, Buddy. Go home and shower now. Matt and I are going to catch some of the ladies' doubles."

Chris and Carol could tell from my face that I wasn't going to come over for dinner tonight.

"Why not?" Chris wanted to know immediately.

"We're going to eat at the Stationhouse with Hans Steger." I said it disconsolately. I was disconsolate. I also knew it was a big name I was dropping.

"Who's he?" Carol asked.

"*The* Hans Steger?" Chris asked. "Tennis World Hans Steger?"

"Yeah," I said glumly. What was she so excited for?

"Who is he?" Carol asked.

"What's he doing in town?"

"He's not in town. He will be. He's in Chicago. They've talked him into stopping here on his way back to Florida. I bet they're paying him plenty."

"All right, both of you," Carol said. "Who is Hans Steger, and what is Tennis World?"

"It's a camp in Florida. He's a great coach, I guess."

"Are you going to hit with him while he's here, Buddy?"

"No, thank God. He's not staying over."

"Why is he coming then?"

"To look me over, I guess. They have an idea I want to go to Tennis World."

"Don't you?" Chris said.

"No. Do you want me to go?"

"Oh . . . no. Of course not. Tell her you don't want to go."

"It's not so easy with my mother."

"That's because you let her push you around all the time."

"Easy, Chris," Carol said. "Even if Mr. Steger weren't

coming to Arborville to meet Buddy, this would still be a big day for Buddy's mother. And—" she hesitated, "not an easy one either."

I wasn't quite sure what Carol meant by that. I guessed it had something to do with my winning a big one and then sharing it first with Chris and Carol. Mom wouldn't be keen on my sharing anything with them. She had already lost Dad to them.

Maybe this was why she was bringing a big gun like Hans Steger to town. To get me away from them. If so, it wasn't really fair. I shouldn't have to pay for what Dad had done. I had known Chris long before he knew Carol. I wasn't to blame for what had happened.

THREE It was almost two years ago that I first met Chris Murphy.

Paul Cotter and I were hitting at the indoor club one November afternoon, feeding each other overheads, trying to see who could bounce one up to the ceiling. It's a stupid thing to be doing, but at the end of two hours of hard practice, it's not a bad idea to do something for fun so you feel like coming back the next day.

Cotter has a big overhead, and he was coming close. Then I hit one that bounced up and hit one of the ceiling joists. It wasn't quite the ceiling, but close enough.

"Hey, I did it," I shouted.

Someone clapped. I turned around. There was this girl sitting on a table off the lounge watching us.

"Good hit," she said.

It was Chris. I knew her name and had seen her around.

She went to a different junior high than I did. She had only started playing tennis a year or so ago, but everyone said she was a comer.

I grinned but didn't say anything. A minute later Cotter was called to the phone. While he was gone, I banged some serves and then walked around the court to pick them up and serve the other way.

"Would you like me to hit them back to you?" Chris asked.

"Sure," I said.

She hopped right down. Quick. But there was no way she was going to hit my big serve back, so I let up and she chipped back returns. This went on for a while until I asked her if she wanted to hit some with me.

"Sure," she said. She was spunky. You could see that right off.

Afterward she thanked me for hitting with her. I said we could do it again if she liked. She said she'd like to but couldn't imagine it would do my game any good. I had won the fourteen-and-under city championships that July, and she was only getting to the top of the intermediates for the fourteen-and-under girls. Fourteen's not young for tennis when you've been playing as long as I have, but I guess it's young to be thinking about girls. Still, I couldn't get her out of my mind.

The next time I was to play Cotter I got Mom to drive me out earlier, figuring this would be Chris's signed-up time. Mom agreed, thinking I wanted extra practice—something she always approved of.

So I got to hit with Chris again, and again, and pretty soon it became a steady thing.

When Dad met Carol it was due to a mix-up. Carol had started giving me rides home from the club. She'd alternate with Mom. One day Carol thought it was her turn and Mom

23

thought it was hers, only Mom was playing in a round robin across town, so she called Dad at the hospital, which isn't too far from the indoor club, and asked him to get us.

Chris and I had just gotten into her mom's car when our old Rambler rambled into the parking lot. It was a '69, the last year they made them.

"That's my dad. What's he doing here?"

You could see the mix-up right away. He was in his hospital gear. He pulled the Rambler up alongside Carol's car.

"Hello, Buddy."

"Dad, I'm getting a ride home with Mrs. Murphy."

"So I see. I'm Dick Berger," Dad said to Carol.

"I'm Carol Murphy. This is my daughter, Chris."

"Hello, Chris."

"Hello, Dr. Berger."

Dad looked us over—me, Chris, Carol—as though he was seeing something for the first time. Then he grinned.

"Who beats who around here anyway?" He was looking at me and Chris.

I felt my face turn red.

"I'm happy to run Buddy home," Carol said.

Dad laughed. "It'll be our turn next time." He gave us a little salute and drove off.

"So that's your dad, Buddy," Chris said.

"That's him. He's pretty busy or he would have taken me home."

"It was very nice of him to come anyway," Carol said.

"Mom should have, but she's even busier than he is."

That sounded cockeyed, even to my own ears, but it was the truth. Tennis, if you're serious, is a lot more demanding than medicine. Which was why Dad gave up being a serious player.

That was the first time Dad and Carol met. A few days

later it was Dad, not Mom, who picked me up at Chris's house.

"Is she a good player?" he asked me later.

"Not really. But she's going to be. She's serious."

"Does her mother play?"

"I've never seen her."

"What's Mr. Murphy like?"

"They're divorced."

"Oh?"

"He lives in California. Chris sees him at Christmas time."

"She's pretty."

"I know. I wish she went to my school."

Only later did I realize he wasn't referring to Chris.

I could tell that Dad liked Carol. But he's good-looking, he was a well-known athlete. Lots of women like to flirt with him, and he flirts back. Mom never minded. So I didn't really think anything about Dad always having a cup of coffee at Chris's house when he came to get me. Or why he even picked me up so much, or gave me so many rides there.

And then one day last March, he came home early from the hospital. Mom was out somewhere, and I was alone, shooting baskets in our driveway. It was the first really springlike day we'd had.

"What're you doing home so early?" I asked him. It wasn't even five o'clock.

"I just killed off my last patient. How about a shot?"

I tossed him the basketball. "Did he go easy?"

"Fought all the way. Stubborn cuss."

He put up one of those silly two-handed set shots that men his age do. To my surprise, it went in.

"I guess I haven't lost the old touch," he said, grinning.

He fed me a bounce pass. I took a jump shot. It missed

Dad tapped in the rebound. He actually looked pretty good doing it.

"You could have been a good basketball player," I said.

He laughed. "I could have been a lousy one too."

"You think I ought to try out for the junior-high team in the fall?"

"If you want to. It'd be a good experience, even if you didn't make it."

I threw up a nice jump shot. "What makes you think I wouldn't make it?"

"It's not a middle-class white sport."

"Black kids are playing tennis."

"They're moving up."

"I could move down."

He laughed and threw up a hook that missed everything except the eavestrough.

"Ugh," he said, "that's enough of that. How'd you like to go over to the park and start the outdoor season with me?"

"Tennis, you mean?"

"Sure. The nets are up. It's a beautiful day. What do you say?"

The day I turned down a tennis invitation from my dad hadn't come yet.

"Sure. But don't you have to go back to the hospital?"

"I'm taking a couple of hours off."

"Gee, Mom would have loved to hit with you too, if she'd known you were coming home early."

"She knows."

"Huh?"

That was the first hint I got, but I didn't understand it till later. I was just so pleased about hitting a tennis ball outdoors for the first time that year and with Dad . . . and at the park.

I loved that old park. We only lived a block from it, and it was a great park. The best in Arborville. It had two ball diamonds, two basketball courts, five tennis courts, and a small hill that was great for sledding in winter, and biking in summer. In winter they made a big rink on one of the diamonds for pleasure skating and they froze the tennis courts for hockey games.

Of course, when you pour a lot of water over a tennis court and freeze it, it doesn't really help the surface. Those courts at Sampson Park were pretty cracked, and there were weeds growing in some of the cracks. The nets had holes in them and there was usually broken glass around from when the burn-outs had their late-night parties. Even when the courts were cleaned up it was still a funny place to play. In summer there was usually a noisy Little League game going on, or kites flying over your head trying to distract you, or kids riding bikes down the hill across the courts. I figured if you can concentrate at Sampson Park you can concentrate anywhere. They were my favorite courts in all the world. It was where Mom and Dad gave me my first lessons . . . and I never minded going back to play there . . . especially with him.

"First court, OK?"

"Sure."

"Let me stretch a little." Dad had been having back trouble. A disc moving and muscles tightening to protect the nerve. He'd get spasms that would lock him up and put him to bed for a week.

"If you did exercises regularly," Mom said one time, "that wouldn't be happening to you."

"Right," Dad replied (the doctor being lectured to), "but I don't have time for exercises."

"It seems to me you have time for other things," Mom said.

Dad was silent. Then he said: "I don't have time for back exercises."

I didn't get it then.

He stretched one leg and then the other and then, legs apart, reached down to touch the ground. But didn't come near it. He groaned. "Buddy, be gentle with me."

That was a laugh. Even out of shape, Dad was one of the top singles players in Arborville. He'd even give a good battle to some of the university's best players.

We went out on the court and hit. The air was cool and the sun was nice and warm on our necks. A couple walking a golden retriever stopped to watch us. You don't often see people hitting with style on a public court.

First outdoor tennis of the year, we didn't play games. Just got used to the air, and how much livelier the ball moved outside. Dad moved me around the court without meaning to. He hit a heavy ball with good top-spin. He had a fine backhand. He really had a complete game.

We stroked and stroked, without talking, and it was a golden time.

Finally he called a halt. "I've had enough."

"You're flabby, Pops."

"You'll be flabby too someday."

"I hope not."

"I hope *so*. If you're not, it means you're a tennis bum and you'll have the flab where it doesn't show."

"Hey, that's deep, man."

"Let's sit down."

I loved that part of Dad. His honesty and kidding and sitting on the grass at Sampson Park like a kid. I guess you're always sort of a kid if you live where you grew up. Dad had grown up on Lincoln Avenue across the park. He'd played here as a kid. He'd learned tennis on these very same courts. Only they were clay then. I wondered if he and I had been kids together whether we would have liked each other. I thought we would.

"Buddy, you're going to be a darn good tennis player."

"Thanks."

"It's due to your mom and Mike Higgins."

"And you."

"I didn't help you."

That should have warned me. The way he had left himself out.

"Hey, you started me. And I've got your tennis genes."

He laughed. "You've got your own genes, son. I never hit a top-spin backhand like that when I was your age. Your mother didn't either. You're your own man, son." He was silent. He looked at me. A warning signal flipped up in my stomach. It was better on the court. Something bad was going to happen here on the grass.

"I want to talk to you about something, Buddy."

"What?"

"Our family."

"Aw, Dad, let's hit some more. I'm getting stiff."

"Sit down, Buddy."

I sat down. I didn't want to, but I did.

"I don't really know a good way to say this. I wanted your mother to be here, but she's angry and. . . ." He couldn't finish.

"What about?"

"Buddy, your mother and I are going to get divorced."

I stared at him. The words hung in the air in front of me like a banner. I could hear a dog barking across the park, and two kids shouting. Someone was flying a kite. It was over our heads, dancing in the wind.

"Things haven't been going well between us for a long time, Buddy. It's not anyone's fault. Not hers, not mine. It's not even a question of fault or right or wrong. It's a question of growing, of time, of two people not being in love with each other any more."

He was talking too fast now. Af first he couldn't say anything, now he couldn't stop.

It wasn't real to me, no matter how much he talked. It was just words. I mean, they were my parents. I'd sat behind them in the car on long trips, listened to them talk, laugh, argue. They were my folks.

"Why do you have to be in love to stay together?" My voice sounded harsh. Why was I even asking him that?

He looked pained. It wasn't working out the way he wanted it to.

"I guess we both still want a lot from life yet," he said. "Buddy, this has nothing to do with Carol."

"Carol? Carol Murphy? What's she got to do with it."

I guess I was dumb. Dad looked surprised. "When the divorce is final," he said, "Carol and I are going to get married."

Carol and Dad were going to get married? Carol Murphy? Chris's mom? Whom he had met through me. This was unbelievable, crazy.

"Hey," I said, "let's hit some."

"No, Buddy, we've got to go through this."

"Sure, sure. I know. But let's hit."

"No," Dad said, "we—"

"Let's play for real, I mean. Let's play a set."

I didn't wait for him to say no, I left him and went out on the court. I felt hot, my heart was pumping. He sat there, and then, reluctantly, he got up and came on the court after me.

"I'm sorry, Buddy. This isn't working out the way I hoped it would."

"You wanna serve?"

"Buddy—"

"We'll spin for it. Tad or Davis?"

"Buddy!"

"Tad or Davis, Dad?"

"Davis."

"It's Tad."

He didn't want to play. He was upset. I didn't want to play either. But I went back and served. I served hard and well. First day out-of-doors and I was playing for my life. My adrenalin was flowing. I was angry. I hated him.

I lost, 6–3.

That was in March. In October they got divorced. In December he married Carol. It was crazy at first, going over there to see Chris and seeing Dad. But I got used to it, and after a while I began to like it. In fact, I liked it more over there than at my house.

Mom knew this, but until I beat Rob Parker and Mr. Hans Steger came to town there wasn't anything she could do about it.

FOUR

FOUR The Stationhouse Restaurant is probably the fanciest restaurant in Arborville. It's also probably the phoniest. It's housed in the old railroad station, and every time a freight train goes by you're supposed to click your fingers. The waitresses all stop work to do it, and so do the busboys. It's real dumb. The kind of thing adults dream up.

But I suppose it's the right place to eat when someone is coming in on the train.

31

Mom and I drove down in the Lincoln. Right away we saw Matt Bigby's red Cadillac. He'd come down early just to make sure there would be no delay after Mr. Steger got there. In fancy restaurants you have to wait forever for your food. Give me a McDonald's anytime.

The maître d', a little bald fat man, came up to us. "Good evening, Mrs. Berger. How are you today?"

"Fine, Harold. Do you know my son, Buddy?"

"Hello, Buddy. Congratulations."

My God, I thought, how would he know about it?

"Thanks."

"Mr. Bigby is over there waiting for you."

"Has he told you we're expecting a guest?"

"Indeed, he has. And he has told me who the guest is. Hans Steger. We are very honored."

Mom smiled. "I didn't know you were a tennis player, Harold."

"I am just starting. This tennis craze, you know. I must keep up with it. My wife is crazy about it, and so I am into tennis now."

Mom laughed. I didn't. I thought it was really dumb how adults used words like "into." I also thought it was dumb that fat, bald men like Harold got into tennis because it was a "craze." Because it was on TV all the time. If hula hoops came back, they'd drop tennis for them.

Matt stood up as we came to the table. He leaned over and kissed Mom. It didn't bother me. But I didn't like looking at it.

"Buddy, you look terrific."

"Thanks."

"It was a little bit over his dead body, Matt, but we made it. How's the train doing?"

"Only ten minutes late out of Jackson."

"His plane leaves at ten-thirty."

"Now don't start worrying, Helen. There'll be time."

"Time for what?" I asked. It sounded like more than worrying about dinner. Though you could spend a lot of time worrying about dinner in a place like this. Just to start with, you could hardly see the menu. The lights were dim. The menu was printed in orange letters on orange paper. It was pretty bad.

"We're going to talk about your tennis future," Mom said, putting on her reading glasses to study the menu.

"What do you mean?"

"Will you be having drinks?" a waitress interrupted us.

"I'll have a whiskey sour," Mom said.

"Scotch on the *rock*," Matt said. "Not much rock either." Then he laughed. He made the same joke every time we ate out.

"Buddy, would you like a Coke?"

"Nothing, thanks."

When the waitress left, I asked Mom again what she meant by my tennis future.

She took off her glasses. "I think it's time to find out how far you can go."

"How're you going to do that?"

"Steger's going to help us," Matt said.

It was "us" again.

"I don't want to go to Tennis World."

"Nobody's offered you the chance," Mom said.

"If they did, I wouldn't go."

"Why not? Some of the best players in the country went there."

"So what? I like it here. You can do OK staying here."

"Soar, Buddy, soar. Fly, Buddy, fly," Mom said.

Matt chuckled. "Maybe we ought to send you to airplane camp too," he said.

I almost smiled.

33

The waitress brought the drinks and wanted to know if we would order now. Mom said it was probably the best thing to do, since Mr. Steger had a plane to make. Then the question became: How do you order for Mr. Steger?

"Risky," Matt said. "Definitely risky guessing what an old man likes."

"Why not order four different things and let him have his pick," I said.

Matt grinned. "Out of the mouths of babes . . . wisdom. Good idea, Buddy."

I resolved to keep my mouth shut the rest of the evening.

They took my advice and ordered a steak, a chicken dinner, a fish dinner, and a chef's salad.

"If he doesn't like one of those," said Matt, "he can lump it."

Every ten minutes he went out and checked the Amtrak schedule—at Mom's urging. She is very compulsive about things. During Matt's last trip to the Amtrak board, a train came in and stayed in. Everyone clapped. (They clicked for the freights that went by and clapped for the train that stopped.) Mom looked excited. "This will be him, Buddy."

"What do I do?"

"What do you mean, what do you do?"

"Do I have to talk to him?"

"Of course you do. If he asks you questions, you answer them."

"I don't want to go to Tennis World, Mom. This summer or in the fall."

"No one's asked you to go."

"If he does, I won't go. I want to stay in Arborville."

"Stop thinking ahead, Buddy. You think ahead too much."

"I don't care. I won't go to—"

"Shsh. Here they are!"

Matt came back through the restaurant escorting a tall old man. You could see right away that Hans Steger had spent a lot of time outdoors. He had a long, leathery face, blue eyes, and lots of wrinkles around them. In those wrinkles you could imagine millions of hours of backhands and forehands, volleys and half-volleys, overheads in the sun. He had played and coached on every continent in the world. He had even gone to Russia to help them set up a junior tennis program.

His camp, Tennis World, was the most famous tennis establishment in the world. It was a combination hotel, camp, college. At a tournament in Lansing once, I also heard it referred to as a factory where players came off the Steger assembly line. It sounded like a rotten place to have to go, even if it was the ticket to tennis greatness in our country.

I didn't like anything about this old man. He was, next to my mother, the hardest-looking person I'd ever seen.

"So," he said, "this is Buddy Berger." His lips smiled, but the blue eyes did not. They bored into me. I was being examined; my emotions were being frisked. It was scary.

Mom said quickly, "Buddy had some good luck today. He beat Rob Parker."

How would he know who Rob Parker was?

But he did. "Parker? I think Rollins recruited him. That is a good victory for a fifteen-year-old. Excellent. How do you feel about it, Mr. Berger?"

No one had ever called me "Mr. Berger" before. What was he up to? I was determined more than ever to keep my mouth shut.

"Buddy's not much of a talker," Matt said quickly. "We've taken the liberty of ordering dinner or else we'd never get you to the airport. We've ordered four different dinners. Steak—"

"The food is not important," Steger snapped. "I did not come here to eat. I came here to talk to young Mr. Berger. What were the scores, please?" He was looking right inside me again.

"Six–four; six–three," Mom said.

Steger looked annoyed. "Mr. Berger," he said, "do you beat Rob Parker often?"

I looked around. I felt trapped.

"Speak up, Buddy," Mom ordered.

"It was the first time," I mumbled.

He frowned. "How do you account for it?"

I didn't answer. This was a pain.

"Come on, Buddy," Matt said. He winked at me. He was trying to relax me, encourage me. "Did you do anything special today?"

Matt didn't know what I'd done. He'd left the match then.

"I don't know," I answered Matt. It was, for once, easier talking to Matt than anyone else.

"Of course you know." Steger's voice was like a knife. It forced me to look at him. "One always knows why one beats someone."

He was right. There wouldn't be many places you could hide from this guy.

"So why did you beat him today?"

"I changed my game."

"How so?"

"I didn't hit out. I mixed it up."

I stole a look at Mom. Her face was blank.

"And it worked?"

"Yes."

"Then it was smart tennis. Winning tennis."

Should I tell Mr. Steger it was all Mom's doing? What would he think of that?

36

"Stand up, please," he said abruptly.

Now what?

I stood up.

"How tall, please?"

"He's just under six feet," Mom said, making me taller than what I was: five-eleven.

"And just starting to grow," Matt said, cheerfully.

Mr. Steger ignored him. "Weight, please, *Mr.* Berger?"

"One twenty-five," I said.

"Give me your arm."

I held out my right arm and didn't dare look around to see if people were staring at us. I wouldn't blame them if they were. There I was, standing in the center of Arborville's fanciest restaurant while a crazy old man was feeling my forearm, my wrist. They probably thought he was a doctor —or a tailor.

"The wrists are good. All right, you may sit down. Mrs. Berger, you are right about him physically. He is impressive for fifteen. And I agree with this gentleman that he will be big."

"Damn big," Matt said, "and I'm no gentleman."

"He'll be quick too," Mom said.

"Will he?" Mr. Steger said, amused. "That's interesting. Most people are born quick. It is interesting that you know that he *will* be quick. And what about the rest, may I ask? What about that which also cannot be taught, nor perhaps even inherited, but is an act of the gods. I mean the wanting, the hunger, the desire, the emptiness . . . is that also on its way, Mrs. Berger?"

Mom's face was flushed. He was baiting her.

He knew, or thought he knew, all about my insides. But there was nothing wrong with Mom's insides.

"Buddy will do fine," she said, flatly.

"Good," he said, and looked at me. "We know what your mother wants, Mr. Berger. Now tell me, what do *you* want? Do *you* want to be a tennis player?"

"I am a tennis player," I said angrily.

That pleased him.

"Good. But I caution you, young man. So are twenty million other Americans. I am speaking about real tennis players. Class tennis players. I am speaking of being one of twenty in the world. I am speaking of tennis eight hours a day, seven days a week, fifty-two weeks a year. I am speaking of competing when the fatigue is on you and the sweat is in your eyes and the other fellow is hitting better than you. I am talking about emptying yourself out for tennis. I am talking about giving up everything for tennis. Are you such a player? Do you want to be one?"

"I ... don't know."

"But you're willing to find out. Good." He turned to Mom. "Will he be going to college?"

"Yes."

"What will he study?"

"We don't know yet."

"Medicine maybe," I said, and everyone looked at me, astonished. I was surprised myself. I'd never said that before. I wasn't even sure I'd ever thought it before. And it was a dumb thing to say to a professional tennis coach. You could go to college on your way to Wimbledon, but you couldn't study medicine on the way. Maybe I was copping out already. What a great reason to become a doctor—because you didn't want to make the sacrifices necessary to play world class tennis.

"Why medicine?" he asked softly.

"My father is a doctor."

"Yes, I know. I understand. Mrs. Berger, you are divorced?"

38

"Correct."

Steger glanced at Matt.

"Does he see his father regularly?"

"Yes."

"Does he play tennis against him?"

He knew about Dad. I felt a quick surge of pride.

"If Buddy wins his semifinal tomorrow and my ex-husband wins his, which he should, they'll be in the finals of our city tournament next Sunday."

Mom's eyes gleamed. She wanted that match-up badly. I felt my stomach turn over slightly.

"Will you beat your father, Mr. Berger?"

"I don't know."

"You might if you think positively . . . aggressively."

"I don't know," I said again, and again he frowned.

He didn't like me. I wasn't the kind of kid he would ever like.

"Mrs. Berger," he said, "I guarantee nothing for your son but hard work and the best competition, day in, day out, he has ever encountered. Let me make it clear that I like your boy. (Liar, I thought.) I like the way he looks, but I do not like how he talks. Naturally, I have not seen him play, but if he has beaten a ranked player like Parker, the talent must be there. However, talent is not always the important factor. How hungry will he be? How much pain will he endure? This I do not know. Perhaps none of us knows this yet. Not even him. So we can find out at Tennis World. I will accept your son as a tryout pupil for one week—Sunday to Saturday. It will be an expensive week, and I promise nothing for him but the best competition in the United States for someone his age. Call me by tomorrow if you wish to send him down next week. Now, there has been enough talk. The food arrives. Let us eat."

Mr. Steger took over the food too. He chose the steak for

me and the salad for himself. He didn't care what Mom or Matt ate. They could, he said, choose for themselves.

five   When Hans Steger said "enough talk," he meant it. Conversation came to an abrupt end while we ate and only resumed while we were waiting for dessert. Then Mom made the big mistake of asking him how he started Tennis World.

The old man's eyes lit up. He told us how it had been an Army Air Corps base during World War II, and how after the war he had gone around the country with a group of tennis players giving clinics and exhibitions to raise money to buy it and convert it to "the finest tennis facility in the world." He mentioned the names of some of the kids who had gone to winter school there. They were the top names in American tennis in the 1970's: Connors, Tanner, Stockton, McEnroe, the Mayer brothers, the Gottfried brothers, Amaya, Fleming, Gerulaitis. He had the number-three-ranked eighteen-and-under player down there right now; he also had the number-one-ranked sixteen-and-under—Rick DeVere, who, like me, was fifteen. I might play him when I went down there.

It wasn't *if*, it was when. I should have been thrilled at that kind of opportunity, but I wasn't. I was just angry at how they'd decided my fate for me, without asking me. Well, I wasn't going. I didn't care what kind of pressure Mom and Matt put on me.

Finally, dinner was over. Matt paid with one of his flashy credit cards, and then it was time to take the big shot to Detroit Metro Airport. Mom asked if I wanted to come along or be dropped off at home.

When she gave me that choice I knew she really wanted

to talk business with Hans Steger and didn't want me around to hear the money part. She knew it would only give me ammunition to turn the whole thing down.

"Could you drop me off at Chris's house? It's on the way out."

I had her and she knew it. Matt promptly proceeded to make things worse. Grinning, he said: "Mr. Steger, what do you do when a hotshot young tennis player has a girl friend he doesn't want to be parted from?"

"I don't have a girl friend," I said.

The blue eyes fixed on me. "Girls and tennis do not go together, young man. When you are fifteen, you are beginning a tennis career. Everything turns toward that. Mrs. Berger, we have no boy-girl problem at Tennis World. We have girl pupils, of course, but we keep the boys and girls separate from each other. Cottages for the boys are far from the girls', and Tennis World is patrolled."

It sounded a little like a prison, I thought.

"That's how it should be," Mom agreed. "You either concentrate or you don't. Buddy, we'll drop you off at home. You need a good night's sleep. You've got a big match tomorrow. Ed Hankins is going to be very tough."

"I know he'll be tough, Mom. I'll be back early."

Mom hesitated. She knew the old man was interested in how she handled me on this.

"All right," she said, "but I want you home by eleven."

"I'll be home by eleven," I promised.

The old man's face was expressionless, but I could tell he thought Mom had made a mistake. She had flunked.

"At Tennis World," he said, "for his age group lights are out at ten P.M."

Matt winked at me.

I rang Chris's bell. She turned on the outside light and

opened the door. We kissed.

"Hmm," she said.

"Hmm, yourself. You're the only girl that turns the light on so everyone can see us."

"How did I know it was you out here?"

"Who else would come calling on you this late? At Tennis World I'd be in bed already."

"Are you going?"

"No."

"For sure?"

"For sure."

"OK," she said. We kissed again. Then she said: "Don't you want to go a little bit?"

"No. Would you?"

"I'd like to see what it's like."

"I know what it's like. It's an old Air Force base patrolled by Doberman pinschers who keep the boys and girls separate and bite you in the behind every time you miss a shot."

Chris laughed. Carol called out: "Who's there, Chris?"

"Buddy."

"Don't keep him waiting outside," Dad said. And then he and Carol laughed.

"Aren't they funny?" I said.

"They think they are. Come on. Your dad wants to hear all about the match against Rob."

"Didn't you tell him?"

"Only the final score."

"That's good enough." I was pretty sure Dad wouldn't approve of my deserting my natural game.

Carol and Dad were sitting at the table with coffee cups in front of them. They had eaten late. Mom and I used to eat late too because Dad always got home late from the hospital. After Dad moved out, we ate at six.

42

"Congratulations, son."

"Thanks, Dad."

"You did the job, I hear."

"I got lucky and he was off."

"I'm sorry I couldn't be there. An emergency came up. Plus Dr. Nielsen called me from New York. They've arrived, and they'll be in Arborville Monday."

"Who're they?"

"It's a Swedish doctor and his family who're going to be here for the coming year. He's going to be on my staff, and Dr. Brandon asked me to kind of look after them all till they get settled."

"In addition to everything else you have to do," Carol said.

"That's all right. I like being busy, though I don't like not seeing my son beat someone as good as Rob Parker. How did you do it?"

"Before we get into that," Carol said, "Buddy, would you like some dessert?"

"No, thanks. We just had a big dinner at the Stationhouse."

"Buddy's not going down there," Chris said.

"All right," Dad said, "let's hear about that first. Hans Steger was really in Arborville tonight?"

"Do you know him, Dad?"

"Not really. He once watched me play in Philadelphia. Tough old bird."

"Was he old then?"

"I think a character like Steger is born old. What did *you* think of him?"

"He's crazy."

Carol laughed. Chris frowned. "How can he be crazy and turn out all the great players that he does?" she asked.

"Chris, if you listen to him talk, you know he's nuts. He

makes it sound like you have to live and die for tennis down there. He talks about hunger and pain and sacrifice and that's all he talks about."

Dad laughed. "That's life at the top, Buddy. He used to talk like that twenty years ago. I'm glad to see some things haven't changed."

"Did he invite you down, Buddy?" Carol asked.

"Yes. For a week tryout."

"That's an honor," Dad said. "Not many are invited for a tryout."

"Tryout for what?" Chris asked.

"Winter school. He's got an all-year-round tennis program that only a few get invited to. The summer camp is supposed to be tough to get into, but winter school is impossible."

"I don't get it," Chris said. "What's winter school?"

"Well," Dad said, "as I remember it from *Tennis* Magazine, Steger has a year-long program down there. He gets the kids enrolled in local schools so they can work out all year round. It's why he calls it Tennis World because that's what it is: Hans Steger's Tennis World."

"How can he send out-of-town kids to local public schools, Dick?"

"I understand he gets power of guardianship from the parents, and since he pays school tax down there, he sends the kids off to public schools."

"That's unbelievable," Carol said. "Imagine a parent giving up a child for . . . tennis. That's tennis adoption."

"Happens all the time. Not in tennis maybe, but in football and basketball. Let's say Chick Watkins, the Arborville High basketball coach, wants a six-foot, nine-inch center from Detroit to come to Arborville High. He finds an 'uncle' for that kid in town here; the uncle adopts him, and six-nine goes to public school here and plays for Chick."

"Dick, I can't believe parents would do such a thing."

"Some six-nine kids in Detroit don't have parents."

"Well, Buddy does have a father and a mother."

"Half a father really," Dad said, and suddenly I realized there was a point behind his half-kidding about the six-nine center. "His mother really controls his life till he's eighteen."

"Dad, she can't send me down there if I don't want to go."

"I'm not so sure about that," Dad said somberly.

"I won't go. Not even for a week. I'm in the middle of a tournament here, just to start with."

Dad laughed. "Let's cross bridges when we come to them, Buddy. As for your being in the middle of a tournament, if you get by Ed tomorrow and I get by Jerry Stoner, our match won't be until next Sunday." He winked at Chris. "I think your friend here could sneak in a quick week at Tennis World and sharpen his game so much he'd trounce me."

"Ha!" said Carol. "So that's why you don't want him to go down there."

"Can you think of a better reason?"

They started to make a joke of it. I've noticed this is a technique adults often use when they come up against something uncomfortable.

Or they change the subject, as Dad did by asking me to tell him about the Rob Parker match. I did, telling him I found a way to help Rob make errors, but I wasn't going to tell him the details in case I had to use those tactics against him in the finals.

Dad laughed. "Fair enough," he said.

I laughed too. Relieved.

Dad and I stacked the dishwasher while the "girls" talked in the living room. Role switch, Dad said. But he really wanted to be alone with me. We talked about Mom and Matt and Tennis World. Dad liked Matt. He always had, he told me. He hoped I wouldn't give Mom an excuse to ship me off to Tennis World. "I don't approve of places like that," he said. "Maybe if you're twenty and wanting a career in professional tennis. But not at fifteen."

"Don't worry. I won't give her an excuse."

Chris and I went for a walk, and right away she wanted to know what Dad and I talked about.

"You. He's worried about your becoming a tennis bum."

"Come on, Buddy. You talked about Tennis World, didn't you?"

"Yeah."

"He doesn't want you to go, does he?"

"Nope. And I don't either. And he doesn't want me to give my mother an excuse to send me there."

Chris was silent. Then she looked up at me. We were walking along Devonshire, which is one of the nicest streets in Arborville. Lots of tall trees and houses set far back and long circular drives.

"You could give her one tomorrow," she said.

"How?"

"By beating Mr. Hankins. Your dad will beat Mr. Stoner easy. And your mom wants more than anything in the world for you to beat your dad. She'd send you to Tennis World no matter what you said, if she thought it would help you beat your father."

I didn't say anything. What Chris said was probably true, but that still wasn't an *excuse* to send me there. It was a *reason*. And a reason wasn't an excuse. My mother wouldn't ever say aloud what Chris had just said.

"You think I ought to lose to Mr. Hankins on purpose tomorrow?" I asked her, and I wasn't sure I was kidding.

"No," she said. "I think you ought to beat him, if you can. And go to Tennis World. And beat your father."

"You take my breath away."

46

"Don't you want to be the best tennis player in the world, Buddy?"

"Do you think I could be?"

"Yes, I do." She said it so firmly that I almost laughed. But she was serious, and she would have been hurt if I laughed. Besides, she looked so pretty. I stopped walking.

"*Numero uno*?" I asked.

"*Numero uno*," she said.

I kissed her.

She and my mother were so much alike. Speaking of which . . .

"Chris, do you have the time?"

"No."

"I promised I'd be back by eleven."

"I don't think it's even ten-thirty, Buddy."

"Maybe not, but I'm not taking any chances. Let's go."

"You know something, Buddy? You're more scared of your mother than of anyone else in the world."

"I'm pretty scared of you."

"Not enough," she pouted.

I laughed. We walked home. We kissed good night, and then I left. Getting home after eleven could be an excuse for my mother. Not much of one, to be sure, but enough for her. My mother could take a little excuse a long way. Like to Tennis World.

I ran all the way home.

six Mom and Dad played their matches at the same time—9:00 A.M. Mine was scheduled for 11:00 A.M. on Dad's court. Dad and Mr. Stoner were to play on Court Number 1, the court nearest the parking lot, Mom on Court Number 5, the far court near the hill.

47

I got to the park about five minutes to nine. Mom was out warming up with Mrs. Willoughby. A lot of women were sitting on the hill to watch the match. Women always watch other women play.

On Court 1, where Dad's match was scheduled, there was no Dad. Mr. Stoner was warming up with a friend.

"Hey, Buddy," Mr. Stoner called out to me, "where's your old man?"

"I don't know, Mr. Stoner. I don't know where they are."

Chris, Carol, as well as Dad, was what I meant.

"That's right. I forgot you all live in different places now." Because Mom, Dad, and I were always around tennis courts, people did sometimes forget Dad went home to a different house.

I let my legs hang over the empty bench in front of me and watched Mr. Stoner hit. He hadn't the big game Dad had, but he could hang in there, and if he ran Dad, that could be the end. Dad would have to get on top of him right away and make Mr. Stoner lose confidence.

Mom and Mrs. Willoughby were just about finished with their warm-up. Mrs. Willoughby is a tall, graceful woman, younger than Mom, with nice, coached strokes. The kind of player Mom eats up with her relentless, attacking game. There's nothing pretty about the way my mother hits a tennis ball. She goes after it, attacks it, hits it hard and always deep and accurately.

More and more people were arriving. It was after nine. Mom and Mrs. Willoughby were toweling off at the net, getting ready. People in the stands began looking at me as though I were responsible for my father's absence.

Paul Donaldson, who runs the tournament for the city, came over, clipboard in hand.

"Buddy, do you know what's up with your father this morning?"

"I don't know. I'm sure he's coming."

"Well, I'll give him a ten-minute grace period because he's second seed and a former champ, but if he's not here in ten minutes, I'm afraid he's got to forfeit. It's not fair to Mr. Stoner."

"Do you want me to go home and call him?"

"No time for that. We better just sit tight."

Down at the far court, Mrs. Willoughby was serving the first game and Mom already had her on the defensive, driving deep to her backhand. The rallies would be long to start with, but then Mom would wear her down and go in and mop up.

"Here he comes," Paul said.

The old Rambler came charging into the parking lot. Dad jumped out in his hospital pants, two rackets in his arms. I thought I caught a faint edge of disappointment in Mr. Stoner. Nobody wants to win by a forfeit unless they know deep down they can't win any other way.

"I'm sorry, Jerry," Dad said. "I had to look in on a patient an hour ago, and I almost didn't get away."

He started leg stretches as he talked.

"That's all right, Dick. Take your time getting ready."

"Buddy, I bet you and Paul were getting worried."

"It's pretty late, Dad."

"Don't I know it?"

"He even wore his tennis shoes to the hospital," Chris said, climbing up to sit with me. "How's your mother doing?"

"They just started. But I think she's winning."

"Dick, where do you want the Gatorade?" Carol asked.

"You sit with it," Dad said. "I don't mind coming over for encouragement as well as nourishment."

How he could crack jokes and be as relaxed as he was, I didn't know.

"Did you go to the hospital with him?"

"Yes," Chris said, "we thought we'd save him parking time. We waited over an hour there. Wow. Your mother really hit that one."

"She's on her game. She was up at six this morning getting ready."

"Was she home when you got back last night?"

"Yes. I just made it in under the wire. No excuses to ship me off . . . yet."

"I wish I could hit an overhead like that."

"Practice for twenty years like her."

"I will."

"Could we get started as soon as possible, gentlemen?" Paul asked Dad and Mr. Stoner.

"Two minutes," Dad said.

"Dad's either going to blow him out or get blown out," I said to Chris. "His adrenalin is flying."

Released from his hospital rounds, Dad was ready to explode in the sunlight. Sometimes it's like that in sports. He was ready to play without really warming up.

Mr. Stoner started serving and Dad went right in and attacked the serve, coming to the net. Dad didn't usually play that aggressively, and it took Mr. Stoner by surprise. Dad was all over the court. Mr. Stoner got flustered. The defensive lobs he put up weren't deep enough, and Dad put them away. Dad kept the pressure up, and slowly Mr. Stoner's game came unglued. Cuts, spins, he threw up all kinds of stuff to break Dad's rhythm, his momentum, his zest, but nothing worked. When you're inspired, you're inspired, and Dad was. He blew Mr. Stoner off the court 6–2; 6–1. It wasn't an upset, of course, but with Dad coming so late, and cold, it should have been a closer match.

At the far court, Mom had put Mrs. Willoughby away even faster. Every time we looked, she'd been winning a point.

50

Her match ended before Dad's. I watched her shake hands with Mrs. Willoughby and then gather her stuff and make her way behind the courts toward the tournament table. She stopped to shake hands with some spectators sitting among the pine trees.

"I'll be right back," I said to Chris. I climbed down and ran around the stands over to the table which was set up near Court 1.

"Congratulations," I said.

"Thanks, Buddy. How's it going here?"

"Dad's giving him a lesson. What were your scores?"

"Love and one."

"Wow."

"She was tight."

"Six–love and six–one," Paul Donaldson repeated, entering the scores on the big sheet. He looked up, smiling. "We could have a bunch of Bergers in the finals."

"I hope so," Mom said. She looked at me. "Have you done your exercises?"

"Yes, Mom."

"You can take Ed Hankins, Buddy, if you bear down. Concentrate."

"Sure."

"Matt's not coming," she said pointedly. I had no excuses now was what she meant. "Limber up a little."

She was on me, coaching, all the time. I didn't have to limber up. I was fifteen years old. I slept limber.

I limbered up.

Mr. Hankins was a gentleman in our warm-up. He didn't try to psych me as Rob had. He treated me as an equal. "Could you hit just a couple more to my forehand, Buddy? I want to check something out."

He was like an airplane pilot with a check list. Forehand,

lobs, overhead, backhand, high backhand. And when he was satisfied, he'd go on to still another item. He asked me where I'd like my balls hit, but I had no check lists. I was as ready as I'd ever be.

He won the serve, and as I walked back to the base line, Mom's eyes sought out mine. I got the message. Get grim.

Mr. Hankins didn't have a hard serve, but he could kick it up pretty high. He got his first one into my backhand. I chipped it back shallow. He was in behind it and put it away cross-court. For an older guy with a little belly on him, he could move in quickly, I thought. There was applause for his quick point.

Well, I thought, if you're going to lose, make him work for it.

I hit his next serve back hard, at his feet, he wasn't in fast enough. He chipped it into the net. Applause for me this time. I knew a lot of people would be rooting for me. Not because they liked me, but because I was fifteen. Ever since Tracy Austin made it into the quarterfinals of the women's U.S. Open, people have been rooting for kids. Though I was no five-foot girl with pigtails. And this wasn't the U.S. Open either.

Mr. Hankins decided to test my forehand. I sliced it back deep to his forehand, forgetting he was a lefty—and then thinking that was OK too. You've got to play your own game, play *your* strengths if you want to beat someone. That's Dad's philosophy, and he's right.

Mr. Hankins started moving me around, dominating me. I'd get a point here and there, but I was playing to his rhythm. He dictated the pace of the game. No matter how hard I hit, or how well-placed my balls were, he always seemed to anticipate them and was there. He won the first set, 6–0, and it wasn't much of a battle.

Mom looked grim. I think I looked grim too, but it wasn't doing any good.

I dropped the first game of the second set and then went to towel off and drink some tea and juice. Mom appeared next to me.

"Hey," I said, embarrassed, "what are you doing here?"

"You've got to change your game."

"I'm working hard."

"I know you're working hard, but you're not going to beat him unless you do things differently."

"Like what?"

"Play moon ball, Buddy."

I stared at her. "Mom, I'm OK."

"You're not OK," she snapped, "he's eating up your stroking. Start hitting them up in the air. The sun's bad. He won't like moving around under it."

Moon ball was how the little kids played in the tournaments. They were scared to win and even more scared to lose, so they smacked ball after ball sky-high, hoping the other kid would give up and overhead one out. The other kid always moon-balled back. And on it went forever. Dad had ordered me never to play tennis that way. Even if it meant losing. "You've got to hit out to win, Buddy. You've got to play strong, natural tennis to win. You'll lose some to the moon-ballers when you're young. But you'll win the big ones when you're older."

"Mom, I can't do it."

"Yes, you can. You will."

"Please, Mom." It was happening all over again, but worse. This time, Dad was present.

"Do it, Buddy. You can beat him that way and *only* that way."

Mr. Hankins came by, changing sides. "Hello, Helen," he said.

Mom nodded at him. There was no cordiality between them. Mr. Hankins was a friend of Dad's.

"Do it, Buddy!" she ordered.

I went to the other court. Dad watched me. I knew he'd been watching Mom talk to me. He didn't say anything. *He* wouldn't.

I got ready to serve.

SEVEN I thought about what Mom said, but I couldn't get myself to do it. And so I went on playing at the end of Mr. Hankins's string. He just ran me all over the court.

And then it happened . . . accidentally. He had angled one deep to my forehand. I knew he was coming to the net. I could have hit a nice lob but instead, and it was almost as though someone had "willed" it off my racket face (and that someone wasn't me), I hit it sky-high, high into the sun. Like a towering pop fly in baseball.

A gasp went up from the crowd.

Mr. Hankins hadn't expected that. He moved a little unsurely, shading his eyes from the sun. A really conditioned player would have had no trouble with it. He would have bounced it and calmly put it away. But I guess Mr. Hankins was thrown off by the nuttiness of the shot. He hesitated and then tried to overhead it. He hit it way out.

Mom nodded to me. I looked away.

Mr. Hankins said irritably, "Try it again, Buddy."

That was a dumb thing for him to say. It meant his emotions could get the better of him. It also meant Mom was right; moon-balling was the only way I could change our match around.

Two balls later I sent up another sky-high pop fly. This one was even higher than the first one. Right into the sun. He bounced it this time and smacked it back hard to my backhand. I sent it back high again, and again, and again, until Mr. Hankins realized—and so did everyone else—that I was going to play moon ball with him in the semifinals of Arborville's biggest tournament.

You can get away with this kind of stupidity if your opponent's not that good and you're willing to run and run. I was willing to run. Quick I'm not, but I've got long legs and I can run.

Run I did, and every time I got to the ball I sent it up sky-high. The sweat began to roll into Mr. Hankins's eyes and slowly, very slowly, his game began to come apart. He missed a few he should have had, and then, out of nowhere, in a moment of anger, he tried to moon one back to me, hoping I'd try to put it away. I didn't though. I was patient. I just mooned it back, the way the little kids do. I calmly let one scoring opportunity after another pass by and seeded the clouds over Arborville with tennis balls.

Mr. Hankins lost his cool.

It's hard to believe a thirty-eight-year-old tennis player will lose his cool to a fifteen-year-old kid, but that is exactly what happened. He was angry at me (I didn't blame him!) and then he got angry at himself for not being able to cope with my game. He couldn't believe I would make fools out of both of us, but that's what I was doing.

And all around the court—complete silence. No one clapped. It was, of course, disgraceful tennis. But it worked. It turned the match around. I won the second set, 6–4.

We stayed on the same sides to start the third and final set and I knew everyone was wondering if, now that I'd drawn even, I would change my strategy and hit out. To tell the truth, I was wondering too. I glanced at my mother. She shook her head. *Not yet*, she was saying to me.

Mr. Hankins served and I returned cross-court. He returned one shallow to mid-court. A good one to angle away and take the net. I moon-balled and dropped back. I could hear the crowd murmur. Mr. Hankins back-pedaled, a little unsteadily. The sun, the sweat, the length of the rallies were beginning to tell on his thirty-eight-year-old legs. He moon-balled it back. I moon-balled back. He smacked a cross-court. I could have tried for a winner down the line. I didn't. I lifted a moon ball to his backhand. I had to beat him in his head. Mom was right. Everything would follow from that. Victory is to the merciless. He should have run around his backhand and tried to put it away, but his legs weren't there any more. He patted it back to me and I sent up a sky-higher that topped all the others. He let it bounce near the base line. It forced him back against the fence. There's not too much room between the base line and the fence at the Sampson Park Courts. Angrily he slammed it into the net.

I won the first game of the third set. I didn't look around at the crowd. I knew what they were thinking. I sat down and was toweling off when Dad said at my right ear:

"Buddy, what the devil are you doing out there?"

He shouldn't be here, I thought. Why can't they just leave me alone?

"Buddy, that's not tennis out there."

"Dad, please stay out of it."

"Buddy, if you win playing this kind of game you'll lose the rest of your life."

"Baloney," another voice said. And now Mom was here too. And right in front of everyone in Arborville they were arguing over me.

"Leave him alone, Dick. He's making a great comeback."

"He's making a stinking comeback, Helen. He ought to be ashamed of himself."

"Dick, I'll never forgive you for this as long as I live."
Mom crouched down. "He's dying out there, Buddy. Keep
hitting them up in the air."

"Buddy, for God's sake, quit hitting those moon balls. Play
your game. You can beat him with your game."

"Are you afraid to face Buddy in the finals, Dick? Is that
it?"

"Damn it, Helen, can't you see what you're doing to him?"

"I'm making a winner out of him."

"You're making a loser. A —"

"Please. Stop. I've got to . . . to play."

I burst between them onto the court. It was humiliating. I
was sure everyone could hear them. They were so wrong to
behave like that, and they were both so right in what they
were saying. I couldn't beat Mr. Hankins with my game.
Mom was right. But it was a shameful way to play tournament tennis. Dad was right too.

But now I couldn't find my real game even if I wanted to.
It was too late to retreat. I had to go on and finish out the
nightmare.

So I served and he returned and I moon-balled and moon-
balled and moon-balled. That final set went on forever, it
seemed. It wasn't tennis. It wasn't a game. It was running
and sweating and staying in it until he cracked. Until he lost
his patience. Which he did. In the end your patience is only
as good as your legs. He stopped trying to keep the ball in
play and he went back to how he had played in the first set,
only he wasn't sharp now. He tried for winners and he
missed.

The dike had broken. My points came faster and faster
toward the end. The last point: I mooned into the sun. He
wanted to hold on, so he lobbed back. Shallow. I came in
and put it away. At least the last point had been a tennis

point. I stayed there at the net waiting for him to come up and shake hands. For one awful moment I thought he wouldn't. He just sagged in the backcourt, breathing in and out, sweat running down his face, and then he walked slowly up to the net and stuck out his hand.

"Smart playing, Buddy," he said.

I wanted to say I was sorry. That it was my mother's idea. But that would have been phony. "Thanks," I murmured.

Mom waited for me at the edge of the court. She held out her hand. "Beautifully played, Buddy."

I nodded. "I better go, Mom. I'm tired."

"I know you don't feel right about it, but you did what you had to do to win. . . ."

I looked up. Dad was gone. So was Carol.

" . . . and that's what tennis is all about."

She wanted me to look into her eyes. She wanted to will me the satisfaction as well as the victory. But it wouldn't work. I didn't want it. There are some games you can't play with yourself.

Not too many came up to congratulate me. None of the juniors came up. Later Cotter would tell me he thought I stunk up the joint, playing that kind of junk game. "At least against Rob you mixed the junk with some good stuff," Paul said. Tom Hannigan, another junior player, said truthfully it was the only way I could have won. Joel Cohen told me he thought I had lots of guts hitting pop flies in the semis.

But Ann Lamson, writing it up for the *Arborville News*, didn't call it pop flies or junk. She called it a "masterful game mixing lobs and soft shots to prolong the rallies and tire the older man." In print it didn't sound so bad.

Mike Higgins shook my hand. "Well, you made it to the finals, Buddy." That was all he said.

And then it was over to the scorer's table to report in

officially to Paul Donaldson. Paul did not congratulate me. He just wrote the score in, and then Mom and I stood alone.

"Buddy, next Sunday it's your father. You won't be able to beat him on moon balls."

"Mom, I'm gonna take a shower."

"This will be the most important week of your life, darling."

"I'm not going down to Tennis World, Mom."

"We'll talk about it later."

"Just so you understand. On the court I'll do what you say because you're always right. But not off of it."

She smiled. "Go home and shower."

"Just so you know."

"Go home and shower."

I left her. Chris met me by the stands.

"Let's get out of here," I said.

"Can I carry something?"

"No!"

"Don't get mad."

"I'm not mad."

"You sound mad."

"I'm just disgusted."

"You won, Buddy."

"It's how I won."

"What's wrong with how you won?"

"Moon balls?"

"Lobs."

"Moon balls!"

"I don't care what you call them, they worked. It's in the record book."

"God, you sound more like my mother than she does."

"I don't care. I know how upset your father is, but he's wrong. You would have lost in straight sets if you'd played your game. There's nothing illegal about what you did. If he had tried to do it to you, you would have beaten him."

"Chris, shut up. You don't know anything."

"I know you won, and that's all that's important."

"Is it? Well now she's making noises about Tennis World. I don't want to go there."

"Well, she can't make you go there."

"She's going to try. I know it."

"Well, don't give her an opportunity, if that's how you feel."

"Chris, don't you see. If she finds an excuse to send me down next week, she'll also try to send me to school there all year round. Do *you* want that, for pete's sake?"

"No," Chris said. "Unless I could go with you."

"Well, you can't."

"Are you saying I'm not good enough?"

I laughed. The tension began to ooze out of me. I grabbed her hand.

"Let's get out of here," I said.

Hand in hand we walked out of the parking lot. I felt my mother watching us go.

EiqHT I didn't feel like talking. Chris understood. She squeezed my hand and we walked silently home.

Coming up our front walk, I heard Snuffy bark. When I unlocked the front door, he was waiting with a rag in his mouth.

"Snuff, man, I'm too tired to play games."

"I'll play tug-of-war with him while you shower."

"My money's on Snuffy."

"It would be."

She grabbed one end of Snuffy's rag and pulled. Snuffy growled and pulled back. Chris made a growling noise right back at him. Snuffy looked at her, puzzled. He hadn't been growled at in years by a pretty girl. But he decided it was OK, because he growled again and shook his head from side to side. Chris giggled. Snuff jerked hard. The rag ripped and Snuffy went over backward.

We both laughed. Snuffy recovered his dignity and walked triumphantly around the room, shaking his end of the rag.

"Come on in, Chris."

I left the front door open. The sun coming through the screen door made a pretty pattern in the hallway. The sun coming through the picture window made a long rectangle on the green carpet. It was nice in the living room. Cool. Our house is set in the middle of a lot of trees. In winter it's cold, but in summer it's just fine. We don't need air conditioning.

On the mantelpiece were some of our tennis trophies. Mom's and mine. Dad had taken his with him.

This was only the third or fourth time Chris had been in our house. Mom never made her feel very welcome.

"There's pop in the refrigerator."

"I'm not thirsty. But you must be."

"No, I'm fine. I'm still a little tight. It's going to take me a while to unwind from that ding-dong match."

"Go take your shower. I'll play with him."

"I won't be long."

As you begin to relax, you begin to feel the weariness in your body that the adrenalin flow masked. Now the emotion was draining out of me, and the lovely physical tiredness, the thing that made all sports wonderful to play, the thing that made you feel honest and clean, was settling in.

I showered, and it felt wonderful. Downstairs I could hear Snuffy barking and Chris giggling. They were nice sounds.

When I got back downstairs the two of them were lying eyeball-to-eyeball in the patch of sun on the carpet. Chris was imitating Snuffy, giving her head little terrier shakes. Snuffy was watching her closely, the way he watches a bee or an ant in front of his nose.

"He's wondering what's the matter with you."

"I don't blame him. How old is he, Buddy?"

"Thirteen."

"Two years younger than us."

"That's human years. In dog years he's ninety-one."

I lay down on the carpet, getting a little bit of the sun, on the other side of Snuffy. He lay in between me and Chris.

"Did you get him as a puppy?"

"Yup. Six weeks old. He was a Christmas present. He's got champions in his family, but he hasn't won any championships himself."

"You don't show him."

"I show him to you."

Chris laughed. "I wish I'd had a dog when I was small."

"Why didn't you?"

"My father didn't like dogs. He was bitten badly when he was a kid, and he never liked dogs."

Snuff got up, stretched, and walked away stiff-legged. Chris and I lay there with the sun on the carpet and the sounds of the nearby street sounding faraway, kids calling to each other, a car going by. Little kids in a backyard running through a sprinkler somewhere in the neighborhood, laughing and shouting. Summertime. The light filtering through the trees. Now the tiredness settling into my bones and feeling so very good and honest. Moon ball and shame were a long way away. It's marvelous how fast you can forget.

"What's your father like, Chris?"

"He's OK."

"Do you like visiting him in California?"

"Yes." Chris never liked talking about her father.

"Why'd your folks divorce?"

She frowned. "I don't know. It happened a long time ago."

"Maybe it's better that way than to have them split when you're old like I am."

"I don't like talking about it," Chris said. "Divorce is dumb. People shouldn't get married if they know they're going to get divorced."

I laughed. "They don't know they're going to get divorced when they marry."

"I bet some of them do. At least they know they can always get out of it. Is your mother going to marry Matt Bigby?"

"He's asked her twice already."

"Why doesn't she say yes?"

"She knows I don't like him. I couldn't live in the same house with him."

"Sure you could."

"No, I couldn't."

"Well, your dad likes him."

"No, he doesn't."

"He says he does."

"That's 'cause he feels guilty about Mom being alone."

Chris looked at me. "Boy, you really have it all figured out."

"Just some of it."

"You think too much, Buddy."

"It's crazy not to think, Chris."

"It doesn't get you anywhere. It just makes you unhappy."

"I'm not unhappy . . . now. I feel pretty good right now." I touched the tip of her nose. The spot where the sweat always formed when she played tennis.

"You know something? You have a very nice nose. I bet you didn't know that."

63

Chris smiled. "Thanks. But your dad is always saying that people with little noses like mine never amount to much."

"That's because he has a big nose."

"So do you."

"Not as big as his. Listen, is that what you talk about at your house? Noses?"

"We talk about lots of things."

"Like what?"

"Why do you want to know?"

"Sometimes I think about it. I mean, it's crazy that he's my father and you're my girl and you see more of him than I do."

"Well, we don't talk about *you*, if that's what you're wondering."

I laughed. It was exactly what I was wondering. I closed my eyes. Let this moment go on forever, I thought, lying here on the rug with no cares, no pressures.

"We talk about his patients. About the residents on his staff. We've spent a lot of time talking about this new Swedish doctor and his family that're coming next week. Mom's supposed to help them find a house and get to know people. We talk about all the bad backs and bad knees in town. I like to listen to your dad talk about injuries."

With my eyes closed Chris sounded faraway.

"Have you figured out yet what to call him?"

"Stop it," she said. I often teased her about that. She wasn't able to call him "Dad." Certainly not "Dr. Berger," and she didn't feel right calling him "Dick." So she didn't call Dad anything. She just sort of caught his eye if she wanted to speak to him. He and Carol knew all about it and laughed at it. They wanted her to call him "Dad." I didn't like that at all.

Chris talked about some lady's knee injury that Dad had found interesting. Or maybe it was her back. Anyway, her voice came from farther and farther away. As though in a dream. And then it wasn't there at all. I guess in that patch of sun on the carpet, I dozed off. Chris must have too.

When Matt's voice sounded in my ears, I was dreaming that I was swimming in a lake up north. Not going anywhere in particular, just swimming.

"Reveille," Matt said. "Everybody up, up, up!"

I opened my eyes. Mom was standing in the doorway. Matt was right behind her, grinning.

"Wow, I must have fallen asleep."

"I guess you did," Mom said, not quite amused.

Chris sat up too. Her face was flushed.

"Chris," said Mom, "I think you better run along home now."

"Mom, we just got here. I was tired and I dozed off."

"Really, Mrs. Berger," Chris said, "I was playing with Snuffy while Buddy showered and then we started talking and—"

"It's no problem, Chris," Mom said pleasantly, "but I do have something I want to talk to Buddy about *alone*."

Chris got to her feet.

"I'll walk you, Chris."

"Matt will take her home, Buddy."

Matt looked surprised.

"She doesn't have to go just yet, Mom."

"I . . . better go, Buddy," Chris said. She looked as though she was going to cry if she stayed another second. "I'll see you later." She ran out the door. Matt gave Mom a kind of warning look, and then he lumbered out after her.

And that left the two of us, as always.

"Why did you do that? We hadn't done anything."

"Go upstairs and wash your face. I want you alert when we talk."

"My face is clean and we have nothing to talk about."

"We have Tennis World to talk about."

I stared at her. So that was her game. How fast she moved when she got the opening.

"I'm not going."

"Yes, you are. Tomorrow morning."

"Why?"

I waited for the phony excuse to come out. But she fooled me. God, she was smart. Always a step ahead of me. Drop shots when I expected drives, cuts when I expected top-spin, down the line when I expected it cross-court.

"Because you're ready for it. You showed mental toughness out on the court today."

Was she laughing at me?

"You proved that you have the discipline, Buddy. Hans Steger can help you. Buddy, darling, you can be a national champion. Not a club champ or an Arborville, Michigan, champion, but a *national* champion. Mike Higgins and I have taken you as far as we can. You're beyond our coaching now. Now you can play for the best coach in America and against the best young players in the world. And that can only happen at Tennis World."

I couldn't believe her pitch. It had nothing to do with Chris then? Nothing to do with my match against Dad next Sunday? Nothing to do with her being alone with Matt for a week? It had only to do with my becoming a national champion!

She looked at me with sincerity. She only wanted it for me. How do you fight that? I couldn't meet her gaze. I looked away. Why was it always forty to love, match point, and her serving?

No, I'd lost every match to her before they ever got started.

I went upstairs and washed my face, which was already

clean. And then she came up and began to lay out clothes for me to take along. Telling me what I needed and why I needed it.

"Can I go over to Chris's tonight to say good-by?"

"I'd rather you got a good night's sleep. It's a four-hour plane ride, and from what he told me last night, you'll be on the courts right after you get there. You can call her up and say good-by."

"Thanks a lot."

But my sarcasm was lost on her as she went about packing my suitcase.

I called Chris after supper. I went into Mom's bedroom to do it. Mom and Matt were talking downstairs. Matt wasn't happy about the way she was hustling me out of the house. Mom told him she knew what was best for me. Matt disagreed, but he couldn't make any more headway against her than I had.

Chris answered the phone.

"I'm going down to Tennis World early tomorrow morning, Chris."

"Oh, Buddy."

"There's nothing I can do."

"I hate her."

"I'll be back next Saturday, Chris."

"Did she think when she came into the house . . . ?"

"I don't know. I don't know what she thought."

Chris was silent.

"Are you there, Chris?"

She began to cry.

"Chris."

"I'll miss you, Buddy."

It was awful.

"I'll miss you too, Chris."

"No, you won't. You'll be meeting new people . . . learning new things. Mr. Steger will invite you to that big winter school right away."

"No, he won't."

She sniffed. "Oh, he will, Buddy. You're good. Everyone knows that except you. Show them how good you are, Buddy."

I smiled. She was such a competitor. Through tears and all. If I had half her heart I'd be a world-beater.

"And Buddy . . . ."

"What?"

"Write me."

"I will."

"Promise!"

"I promise."

It was time to say good-by, and neither of us knew how to do it. And then Chris did.

"I love you," she said. She'd never said that before. I'd never said it to her. They were words you heard on TV, read, but they were hard coming out of your mouth if you were honest. And Chris was honest, and so was I.

"I love you too," I said, and then we hung up—together.

I went back to my room and turned on the radio and turned the dial till I found the wildest rock station in Detroit, and then I blindly grabbed a book off my shelf. It was a book that didn't go with the rock music at all. Which was OK, since I wasn't going to read the words anyway.

"Pity has no place in tennis. Love is only a score."

—Hans Steger
Tennis World
Sun City, Florida

II. Florida

NINE

TENNIS WORLD
SUN CITY, FLA.

Those were the faded letters on the old wood station wagon waiting for me at the airport in Jacksonville. At least I thought it was waiting for me. The driver, a guy in a baseball cap, leaned against the car reading a newspaper.

"Excuse me," I said.

The top of the newspaper lowered a couple of inches and blank eyes looked at me and then at my tennis gear.

"Yeah?" he said.

"My name's Berger, and I'm on my way to Tennis World."

"That so?" The paper raised and he went on reading. What a welcome.

"Are you leaving for Tennis World?" I asked.

"In a while," he said, pronouncing *while* like "waahl."

"Could I go with you?"

It was like pulling teeth. But maybe that was the South. I'd never been in the South before.

"Mebbe," he said, reading.

I just stood there, not knowing what to make of it. Then above our heads a big jet descended. A colorful Braniff jet.

The newspaper lowered again. The driver looked at the plane. "Thet'll be Rick," he said.

"Rick?"

"Rick DeVere. Thet's who ah'm waitin' fur."

"Oh."

Although I didn't know it, it was lesson number one at Tennis World: Cars for Stars.

A few minutes later a stocky, dark-haired kid came out of the terminal. He was carrying a bunch of rackets under one arm and hauling a Suit-Pak over his other shoulder. I recog-

73

nized Rick DeVere's face from *Tennis* Magazine. It was a handsome, cool face.

"Hello, Danny."

"How'd you do down theah, Ricker-boy?"

DeVere winced. "I lost to Costello in the finals. That's how I did down there." He looked at me, at my rackets, and then back up at my face. I could see him wondering if he knew me or not. And then deciding he didn't, and that was OK too. He grinned. "Going to camp, pal?"

I nodded.

"Hop in then." He tossed his stuff in the back of the wagon. I did likewise. He climbed into the front seat. I got in back. He turned and stuck out a hand.

"Rick DeVere."

As though I didn't know.

"Buddy Berger."

"Where're you from, pal?"

"Michigan."

"How long you down?"

"Just a week."

"Tryout week?"

"I guess."

"You must be OK then. The old man doesn't usually let people down in the middle of camp for one week. Unless they're good. Right, Danny?"

"Or rich," Danny said.

DeVere laughed. He looked back at me. "Which is it with you, pal?"

"Probably neither."

"Oh, oh. Modest type. Type we got to look out for. Right, Danny?"

Danny drove us out of the airport. The back of his scrawny neck was red and lined. He was chewing gum. The sides of his jaws moved rhythmically.

"Old man's gonna be sore at you for losin', Ricker."

"Aw, shut up," Rick said. He turned to me. "You playing any tournaments this summer?"

I made my first mistake. "I'm in the middle of one back home right now."

"You're kidding."

I made my second mistake. "Well, not exactly the middle. I'm in the finals. They want to play the final next Sunday so they can get a crowd."

"That's a cushy setup. I never heard of anything like that unless it's a TV deal. Who're you playing?"

And then I knew I'd talked too much. "Oh . . . you never heard of him."

"Hey, man, I won the Kalamazoo Invitational this spring."

I remembered that he had. I'd gone to K-City in April and been knocked out in the first round. I hadn't stayed to watch any of the other matches. My mother drove me home promptly—and silently. It was an early tournament. A kid from Indianapolis had beaten me playing a steady-eddie game.

"Well, this is just a dinky city tournament."

"Yeah? What city?"

"Arborville."

"That's where the university is, ain't it?"

I nodded.

"Drove through there. Played against someone from there once. Can't remember his name. Older kid. He sliced a lot. What's your man's name?"

He meant my opponent.

"You . . . wouldn't know him."

"Try me, pal."

"Well . . . ." I was embarrassed now. "It's my father."

"You're kidding."

"No."

75

He laughed. "You hear that, Danny? This dude is playing his dad in the finals of a tournament."

"Mebbe it's a family tournament," Danny said, and they laughed together in the front seat.

"He's pretty good," I said, trying to stop the anger rising in me. "He was ranked nationally in college."

"Yeah? What's his name?"

"Dick Berger."

"Never heard of him. How old are you?"

"Fifteen."

That did stop him. He looked at me carefully. "You're big."

"I know," I said.

He shrugged. "That's OK. The big ones fall harder. Except for that damn Costello. I'm telling you, Danny, that cat had a reach on him."

"Tim Costello?" I asked, not really believing that was the Costello he was referring to. Tim Costello was seventeen, a member of the Mexico Davis Cup team. *Tennis* Magazine ran a big story on him last winter because he had an Irish father who was a horse trainer and a Mexican mother who was a ballet dancer. I'd seen him play on "ABC's Wide World of Sports."

"Yeah Tim—south-of-the-border—Costello. You ever play him?"

"No," I said, matter-of-factly, as though it were even a possibility.

"I beat the louse in the Easter Bowl in March, but he was too tough yesterday. Hey, Muldoon, who told the old man?"

"You didn't call him, Ricker, so he figgered it out for hisself. Then he called Houston to get the scores."

DeVere laughed. "The old bugger's got to know everything, don't he? Well, Michigan, you'll either love it or hate it down here. It's a meat grinder and we're the meat. Meat in the heat. But we have fun too, after the old man goes to bed. Don't we, Danny boy?"

"Some do and some don't," Danny Muldoon said.

Rick winked at me. "Danny's a little scared he'll lose his cushy job if I tell you how he fixes us up at night. After the old man hits the sack, that's when camp starts bouncing. And Mister Muldoon here, he's chief bouncer. Ain't that right, cat?"

From the back of his skinny red neck, I knew Danny Muldoon was flattered. But he didn't answer.

"Anything new in camp this week, Dan?"

"I picked up a chick from California last night and drove her in."

"What's she look like?"

"She ain't played yet, Ricker. I figger the old man's gonna run her this afternoon. Mebbe with *him*." He jerked a thumb back at me.

We were on an interstate now. Barreling along pretty fast, the station wagon making lots of rattling noises. It could have made a pretty good percussion section for our junior-high-school orchestra.

"Danny," DeVere said, winking at me, "I don't mean her tennis. What's she *look* like?"

"The way you like'm, Ricker. Small."

"That's good. This camp's full of tall tennis chicks. OK for you, pal, but I like'm small."

"I've got a girl back home, Rick."

"So do we all, pal. We all got girls back home, but camp is somethin' else. You got to relax. The old man puts the pressure on."

"But he told my mother there was no fooling around with girls down here."

DeVere and Danny Muldoon burst into laughter. They

77

didn't even answer me. In fact, they ignored me the rest of the ride. They talked about the new girl whose name was Ross. Everyone, I'd find out, was called by their last names in Tennis World. She lived in "Alice Marble House," whatever that was, and Muldoon would arrange a party tonight.

"Which I sure do need," DeVere said. "I lost ten pounds in Texas. The old man better go easy on me."

"He'll be sore you lost."

"That's OK. I am too. But we'll work around him, won't we, cat?"

Danny's fingers beat a tattoo on the steering wheel. DeVere relaxed in his seat. "I'm glad to be back," he said, as we rolled along the interstate to Tennis World.

TEN Tennis courts . . . tennis courts . . . tennis courts. More than thirty of them backing into each other. Mostly clay, but some composition and some cement. And on the courts, kids of all ages in white shorts and shirts, stroking balls under the watchful eyes of instructors.

On still other courts, machines projected balls; one even shot lobs into the air for volley and overhead practice.

Surrounding the courts were rows of small cottages, making it all look like a subdivision on the outskirts of a city. On one side were the girls' cottages; on the other side, separated by the courts and a small pond, the boys' cottages.

"You," said the woman behind the clubhouse desk, "are in Ellsworth Vines House." She handed me a key. And when I looked blank, she explained to me that the cottages all had names. The girls' cottages were named after famous women players like Helen Wills Moody, Alice Marble, Maureen

78

Connolly. The boys' cottages had names like Bill Tilden House, Rene LaCoste House, Don Budge House, and mine —Ellsworth Vines House. Whoever Ellsworth Vines was.

"Both your roommates are playing tournaments out of town, Mr. Berger, so you have a cottage to yourself. Here is a list of the rules of Tennis World. Mr. Steger is very strict about the rules. Lights are out at ten P.M. for your age group. This is the weekly schedule. Please post it on your bulletin board. A daily schedule is handed to each student at breakfast. This is yours for the rest of today. You will notice, Mr. Berger, that you are on center court—Court Number One—at four P.M. with Mr. Steger. All new students always play with Mr. Steger upon arrival at Tennis World. Your set will be videotaped and played back at tonight's think session. It will be only a three-game set, since there is another new pupil in camp today. I am not certain which of you will play Mr. Steger first, so be there promptly at four P.M. . . ."

Her voice droned on. I stood there in the large, airless clubhouse room while overhead an old-fashioned wooden propeller fan whirled slowly, trying heroically to push the heavy Florida summer air around. There was no air conditioning. Through the screened windows I heard the sounds of tennis balls being smacked back and forth. The station wagon went by, with Danny Muldoon driving. Somewhere Rick DeVere was probably explaining his loss in Houston to Hans Steger.

"You will notice that dinner is promptly at six-fifteen P.M., the woman went on. "It is jacket, shirt, and tie for boys. No tennis shoes are allowed. The rules at Tennis World are designed to promote superior people as well as superior players. Mr. Steger believes that if you are to play the tournament circuits you must know how to live in that world. Ellsworth Vines House is in the first bank of cottages on your left. It is the end cottage right after Little Bill Johnson House. Good luck."

I hoisted my suitcase, got my rackets together, and set out to find Ellsworth Vines House.

As I marched by the courts, some kids playing glanced at me. I thought I got some half-pitying grins.

The cottage before mine had a small sign on it that said "Little Bill Johnson House." I'd have to remember these names to ask Dad.

Sitting on the steps of "Little Bill Johnson" were two kids who looked about my age. They had towels around their necks. One kid was tall and thin, the other a roly-poly type. They looked me over carefully as I came by.

"Norton, old chap," said the tall, thin one, "I do believe there's new meat in camp."

"I believe you're right, Carmody," Norton said. "I believe it arrived in Muldoon's wagon with DeVere."

They were talking about me as though I were deaf or didn't exist. I kept on walking until Norton said: "Welcome to Tennis World, new meat."

I let my suitcase down on the hard, red dirt. "Hi," I said.

"How did the great man do in Houston last night?" Carmody, the tall one, asked.

"He lost."

They both cheered, clapped hands, and whistled.

"You look surprised, new meat," Carmody said. "Wait till you get to know DeVere better."

"To know him is to hate him," Norton said.

"I'm Tom Carmody from Boston. This fat kid is Oliver Norton from Northbrook, Illinois."

"I am not fat," said Norton. "I just look fat. What's your name, new meat?"

"Buddy Berger. I'm from Michigan."

"My cousin Ray won a tournament in Detroit two years ago," Oliver said. "Ray Norton."

I shook my head. I knew what was coming now.

"Do you know Todd McHale from Grosse Pointe?" Carmody asked.

I shook my head.

"How about Len Samuels from Southfield? I played him in Indianapolis this spring."

"Norton, what was the name of that drippy kid from Detroit who was here at the beginning of the summer?"

"Wakefield."

"No, he was from Ohio."

"Littlefield."

"No, he was from . . . ."

And on they went with the name game. Finally they realized I wasn't playing and that I probably didn't know anyone. Carmody asked me how I got here anyway.

"I beat a Midwest-ranked eighteen-year-old the other day."

Carmody whistled. "You're down here for a winter school tryout then."

"Next stop Wimbledon," Norton said.

"He only picks ten for winter school. DeVere's winter school. Norton and I couldn't even come close."

"We're even lousy summer players."

"Correct. The only reason we're down here is that our folks hate us and don't want us around."

"My folks don't hate me, Carmody," Norton protested. "They don't want me around, but they do *not* hate me."

"Well, I can tell you why they don't want you around. You snore too loud."

"I don't snore at all."

"Stay awake sometime and listen."

I laughed. They both looked at me sourly. Carmody said: "Lefferts and Dunn, your roomies, are out of town this week. You're pretty lucky to have a cottage alone. Of course, that means we have to have the party there."

"What party?"

"Party for new meat," Oliver Norton said. "I'm going to invite the new girl that came in yesterday. The one from California. What's her name again, Carmody?"

"Ross."

"I think she's my type. Anyway, she doesn't look like a tennis player. She looks soft."

"Wait till DeVere sees her."

"Maybe I can hide her."

"Not if the old man plays her this afternoon. You're on the killing ground too, aren't you, Berger?"

"You mean the match with Mr. Steger?"

"Around here we call him Hans."

"Behind his back."

"I once said it to his face," Norton said.

"But you were a mile away downwind when you said it."

"That's true. But it was still brave of me."

"What's this match all about?" I asked them.

They grinned at each other.

"Hard to describe, wouldn't you say, Norton?"

"Impossible."

"And the afterward. That's when the match really starts. But we make it up to the victims, don't we, Norton?"

"In the after-afterward."

"That's the party, Berger. The big party in your cottage."

"He told my mother that boys and girls were completely separated here at Tennis World." I had asked DeVere about this, but I wanted to get another point of view. I didn't. I got the same one.

82

"We are until the old louse goes to bed. And that is when the mice come out to play. Don't we, Carmody?"

"And the rats, Norton."

"Well, maybe old Rick won't come to her match today. He's so stuck-up, maybe he won't even know she's here. And I could be in so solid with her by the party that—"

"Do not count on it, Norton. This is Ricky-Ticky's world and what Ricky-Ticky wants, Ricky-Ticky gets. Unless young Berger here can slay the wicked dragon. What do you think, young Berger? Can you slay the wicked dragon DeVere?"

I thought the two of them were funny but sad. I wondered how good they were. Real tennis players didn't jaw the way they did. I hoped I wouldn't turn into guys like that. I hoisted my suitcase up.

"Ta, ta, dragon-slayer," Oliver Norton called after me. They were laughing as I passed out of earshot.

Ellsworth Vines House was a plain cottage with a fancy name. Ellsworth Vines's picture faced me as I entered. A big dude in long white pants holding a couple of rackets across his chest. Posing. Somewhere like Forest Hills. A sea of faces behind him. Below his left foot: "To Hans Steger with best wishes—Ellsworth Vines. September 1928, Forest Hills."

Wow. I'd have to look this guy up in the record book. And if Hans Steger played against him, how old did that make Steger? It was mind-boggling!

I looked around the cottage. There were three beds, three desks, three chairs, three standing lamps, three table lamps on the desks, three small bureaus for clothes. It really was army style, like its history.

I looked at the desks of the roommates I'd probably never meet. On each desk was a picture of a girl. Pretty girls in tennis clothes.

Well, I'd put Chris's picture up too. She was as pretty as

their girls. Maybe prettier. And I'd write to her. Not yet though. I wanted to get a feel for the place before I wrote. If I wrote now it would be how lousy I thought it was. People like DeVere. The two clowns next door. The strict rules that didn't seem so strict after all. So I didn't write right away. Which, looking back on it, was probably a mistake.

I got changed. I wanted to be ready for my match with Mr. Hans Steger. Whatever that could possibly be like.

ELEVEN When I got to Court 1 at Tennis World I knew how the Christians must have felt in ancient Rome when they arrived at the Coliseum.

There was a big audience of tennis players waiting to look at the latest shipment of goods from the provinces. Oliver Norton and Tom Carmody were there, but I didn't see Rick DeVere, which was a break.

A girl was sitting on the bench next to the umpire's stand. She was small and pretty. She also looked unhappy as she sat there twisting and turning a racket in her hands. She looked at me as I sat down near her.

"Hi," she said, her voice barely managing it.

"Hi."

There were lots of comments from the crowd. Like:

"Lovely couple, aren't they?"

"Alligator bait."

"Mixed-up doubles at best.

"Wait till the old man gets hold of 'em."

The girl's knees were shaking. "Do you know which of us plays first?"

"No."

"I don't think I can hit a ball. I'm scared."

84

"You'll be all right."

"No, I won't. I'm no good anyway. And with all of them looking at me, I'll be worse. What's that?"

Danny Muldoon, the driver, had arrived pushing a cart with a small TV camera and recorder on it.

"That's videotape."

"Oh, God."

"Don't you get taped back home?"

"No. I'm no good there either."

I laughed. "If you're no good, how come you're here?"

"My older sister came here. She's Cindy Ross."

"Oh."

Cindy Ross played on the women's pro tour.

"My folks think I could be as good as her, but I can't. And I don't want to be. I didn't want to come here. I'm so scared right now. Look at my knees shake. I won't even be able to stand up."

"You'll be OK." Whatever nervousness I had felt was quickly disappearing. This girl was scared enough for both of us.

Danny Muldoon plugged his recorder into a metal outlet. Then he plugged the camera, which was on a tripod, into the recorder. This was familiar stuff to me. Mike Higgins video-taped all his pupils for playback sessions.

"Would you go first?"

"If he'll let me."

"I'm afraid of him."

"He *is* pretty scary."

"Thanks. Thanks a lot."

I laughed again. The girl was making me feel real loose. I couldn't believe she was as bad as she made out. She came from a tennis background.

Suddenly the noise from the stands stopped. The Lord

High Executioner himself—Mr. Hans Steger—emerged from the clubhouse and was now descending the steps toward the courts. He wore long white linen pants, like Ellsworth Vines's, a white shirt, and he carried two rackets. Only they weren't old-fashioned rackets. They were modern metal.

On second thought, his wasn't the walk of an executioner. It was the walk of a god. The God of Tennis World. He didn't look left or right. He didn't look at us as he stepped onto the court. He walked over to the camera and asked Danny Muldoon if everything was in order.

"Yep," said the ever-talkative Muldoon.

"Record the warm-ups," Steger ordered. "Miss Ross, you will take that side, please."

"Good luck."

"I can't get up."

"Yes, you can."

"I can't. My legs are paralyzed."

I gave her a hand up. She wobbled. Someone laughed. Steger glared at the stands. The laughter died.

"Be tough," I called after her.

But she wasn't very tough at all. From the moment Steger put the ball in play, you could tell the girl didn't have it. She was well-coached, you could practically *see* the lessons, but she had no body, no oomph to her strokes. It had nothing to do with nerves. It just wasn't there. This poor kid had been shoved into tennis. I felt sorry for her.

She and Steger warmed up for about ten minutes. Steger moved her around the court methodically. I got interested in watching him. He had short little old-man's strokes, wristy, as in badminton or squash. But they propelled the balls to the exact spots he wanted. He brought her up to the net with a drop shot and then fed her balls gently, making her stretch more and more until one went by her. He smiled at her, but there was no warmth in that smile. He had seen everything. There were no secrets. The "match" was only a formality.

"Are you ready, Miss Ross?"

The girl nodded. She looked at me. Being a fellow victim had made me a friend. I made a little fist at her. *You can do it*, I tried to "will" her. *Get tough. Play hard. Concentrate!*

Roles were reversed. I was my mother and the scared girl out there was me.

Hans Steger addressed the crowd. "I am pleased to introduce Miss Nancy Ross from Santa Barbara, California. Miss Ross's older sister, Cindy, was, as many of you know, a quarterfinalist at the Open last year. I will be playing a three-game set with Miss Ross. Mr. Farrell, new balls, please."

A tall instructor had come up behind the bench—Tom Farrell. He played number three at Stanford, which was like playing number one anywhere else.

Steger told the girl to serve. She took six practice serves: three from the forehand side and three from the backhand. Not one of them did she hit very hard.

Then the set, if you could call it that, began. It was a teaching set. Steger was out to test every part of her game, including her mental attitude. He moved her around the court, side to side, up and down, lobs for her overhead (she didn't have one) and dink shots to see what she could do with an easy ball at mid-court (nothing).

Like any coach playing with any pupil, Steger was also playing to win. No one ever likes to lose. Even a "teaching" game. And at her advantage in the second game, he hit a couple of hard shots down her backhand line. She watched them go. She didn't try for them. He frowned. The TV camera took it all in.

He let her win one game and then he took the last game, a drawn-out affair in which he ran her in circles. He won the last point when she hit a ball into the net. She stood there, not realizing it was all over.

"Thank you very much, Miss Ross," he said, advancing to the net and holding out his hand.

She ran up, shook it, and then ran off the court and sat down on the bench and looked down at her racket. One person clapped and one person laughed. And that was the only reaction from about a hundred spectators—all hotshot young tennis players.

"Hey," I said, "you did fine."

"I was terrible."

"No, you were OK. You've got good strokes. You—"

I stopped. I wasn't doing her any good. In fact, I might have been making it worse, for a tear had formed at the corner of each of her eyes.

"Mr. Berger!" Hans Steger's voice shot through the air.

"Yes, sir."

"We're waiting for you."

Snickers.

Anger swept into my body. I walked out onto the court, and when Steger put a warm-up ball into play I slammed it back at his feet. He couldn't handle it. Or the next one, which I hit at him so hard it almost hit him in the stomach.

Warm-up? The snickers ended. Steger looked at me curiously before putting the third ball into play. I had surprised him. I was obviously coming on differently than he had expected.

The anger on behalf of Nancy Ross was also on behalf of myself—another victim to tennis. And that anger stayed with me through the warm-up. I creamed every ball he hit at me. And they were good shots too. Accurate as well as hard. He just let them go by. The result, of course, was that neither of us was getting a proper warm-up. But he didn't need one. He'd just got through playing. I did though. I'd been

88

four hours in an airplane. Now I was on a tennis court. And here I was wasting my time. Not to mention my mother's money.

By the time I realized how stupidly I was behaving, Steger had had enough. He told me to take six serves, which I did, and then he held up his hand to the crowd.

"I am pleased to present to you Mr. Buddy Berger from Arborville, Michigan, who will be a pupil here for this week in sixteen-and-unders. He is also a candidate for winter school, having recently defeated a Midwest-ranked eighteen-and-under player—Mr. Rob Parker. Mr. Berger will serve first."

My anger was all gone. I thought hard. I hadn't let him probe my game in the warm-up. I had better let him do it now in the short set. I wouldn't lose to an old man like him, but I'd let him move me around.

So instead of hitting a hard first serve, I sliced one down the middle of the box, shallow and friendly. He looked surprised, and then wristed it deep to my backhand. I sliced back to him in the middle so he wouldn't have to move for it. He drop-shot to my forehand. I anticipated and put it away down the backhand line. He didn't try for it.

And so it went. I never once hit it as hard as I had during the warm-up, or made him run for it. If he was grateful, he didn't show it. He played with a poker face. Our games unfolded in absolute silence. No one clapped for a winning point. No one talked. The TV camera followed my every move, remaining on even while I waited for his serve. I beat Hans Steger, 3–0, but we were on the court almost twenty minutes because I wanted to let him probe my game.

After the last point Steger came up to the net and we shook hands.

"Thank you, Mr. Berger. Your match will be analyzed after dinner. In the morning your instructor will be Mr. Farrell. In the afternoon you will participate in the round robin for your age group."

And he walked off the court. I went back to the bench. Nancy Ross looked up at me wonderingly.

"You're good," she said.

"We'll find out tonight at replay time."

"Oh, you won't have to worry. You beat him three–love."

"I'd guess a lot of kids here do that."

"I didn't."

"Boys . . . not girls."

"I just dread . . . ." she hesitated. "Well, I guess I better go. I hope I see you later."

"Me too."

"Are you eating with anyone? I mean, I don't know anyone here at all."

"Me neither. I don't even know where we go to eat."

"It's that brown building there. The long one."

"Would you like to eat together?"

She nodded.

"I'll meet you there then."

"Inside or out?"

"Inside."

She smiled. "Thanks. I'll see you later."

I watched her go, walking timidly around a knot of players who grinned after her.

I left too, but I hadn't gone ten steps before Carmody and Norton fell in on either side of me.

"You've got a nice game, Berger," Carmody said.

"Very nice," said Oliver Norton.

"But don't expect flowers tonight."

"I don't."

"Why didn't you hit like you did in the warm-up?"

"I stopped being sore."

"What were you so sore about anyway?"

"How you all treated her."

"She's a terrible player."

"That's not the point."

"Down here that is the point. The point of everything."

"Then it's all wrong down here, Carmody."

"Listen to him. Been here two hours and already knows what's wrong and what's right. Look here, Berger, this is a tennis camp. And you never mix up tennis with anything else . . ." he grinned, "until after the old man has gone to bed. Then your little bird will get all the attention she wants."

"From me too," Norton said, beaming.

"And from DeVere once he spots her. Once DeVere sees little Ross he'll want that for himself. And then you'll have your hands full, Sir Berger. Then maybe you'll get mad all over again and slay the wicked dragon and make the world a better place for all of us."

Norton giggled. Carmody slapped me on the back.

"You're both nuts," I said, and speeded up, leaving them behind in the late afternoon sun.

I lay down on my cot in Ellsworth Vines House and stared at the picture of the cool Mr. Vines. He looked like he never got angry on a court. Just picked up one championship after another.

Overhead a fan whirred. It was hot in the cottage. All the afternoon heat had settled in and stayed. Like an oven. I was sweating more lying here than I had on the court. Or maybe I was just more aware of it now. I probably ought to get up and shower, and change. I was eating with Nancy Ross. I wasn't being disloyal to Chris. Ross and I were fellow victims today. With her more victimized than I. I shuddered to think what they would do to her tonight.

TWELVE Walking up the red clay camp road—it must have been at least a hundred degrees out—I felt stupid all dressed up.

But wherever you looked there were kids walking up camp roads in jackets, shirts and ties, good pants, and street shoes. And across the way, on the girls' side, they were wearing skirts and blouses. No blue jeans or sneakers for them either.

Later Tom Farrell explained to me that for Hans Steger dressing for dinner in the summer heat had a double purpose. "First of all," Tom said, "the old man believes in pain as a matter of principle. If you can live and play through pain then you have a chance of making it to the top. Then, if you make it to the top, you'll find yourself being hosted by all the top people around the country, so at least you already know how to dress for dinner and use a knife and fork."

I had to admit Steger's system had a certain logic to it.

By the time I got to the dining hall—which was halfway up the hill behind the clubhouse and had a nice view of the courts, the cottages, the small pond beyond the courts, and the main highway to Jacksonville off to the south—almost everyone was inside eating.

I looked into the dining room. There were individual tables set up, and each table was set with a tablecloth and a little lamp. There were usually four boys and four girls at a table, but some tables had two boys and two girls. And one table I spotted had two boys and one girl. The boys were Carmody and Norton. The girl was tall, I guessed the one Norton was teasing Carmody about. Carmody saw me and gestured for me to come over, pointing to the empty chair. I shook my head and went back into the entrance hall.

I studied the bulletin board there. Lots of notices: racket

restringing hours, prices for gut and nylon. Someone wanting to trade a TAD Davis for a Bancroft; someone missing "my favorite sweatband with my favorite smell"; someone wanting a ride to Valdosta, Georgia, next week. . . .

There were the results of different camp tournaments posted. DeVere's name wasn't listed on any of them. He'd be on the travel team. The kids who won the camp tournaments were probably not the best players in camp. The best players in camp went out during the week to play around the country. I wondered if their folks paid more or if the also-rans paid for the top players' trips.

"She's inside," a voice said behind me. I turned. It was Oliver Norton.

"Who's inside?"

"Ross. DeVere latched onto her, like Carmody told you he would."

I didn't believe him. He beckoned, and I followed him to the doorway, and he pointed. Nancy Ross and Rick DeVere were sitting at a table.

"You see," Norton said, "that's the way he is. We saw the whole scene. She was waiting here for you. He practically dragged her in."

I didn't believe that.

"What are you going to do about it?" Norton asked me.

"Nothing. It's a free country. She can eat with whoever she wants."

He looked disgusted. "You'll let him do what he wants too, won't you?"

"Oh, come off it, Norton. He didn't drag her in. I don't believe that for one second."

"Well, you should have been here. Want to eat with us?"

To tell the truth, I didn't want to eat with anyone. But I guess you had to eat with someone, so I said OK, and we went into the dining room. I got halfway across the room when Nancy Ross called out to me.

"Buddy, we're waiting for you."

And it was true. They hadn't gone to the buffet yet.

"Don't let him get away with anything, Berger," Oliver Norton whispered.

I wished those guys would fight DeVere for themselves. I wasn't going to fight him. He had nothing to do with me.

I walked over to Nancy Ross's table. DeVere lounged there, grinning cockily at me. "Hello, old pal."

"Hello, Rick."

"Do you two know each other?" Ross asked.

"We came in together from the airport."

"I was wondering what happened to you."

"I guess I took a while showering."

DeVere winked at me. "You don't mind my joining you, pal, do you?"

"No," I lied.

"Good. I figure you and Ross might need a little help tonight."

"Rick's been scaring me," Nancy Ross said.

"Just telling it like it is," he said and laughed. "Come on, let's get some food."

We followed him to the buffet.

"I'm sorry," Nancy whispered to me. "He was just so . . . insistent."

"I know. He runs the place."

DeVere heard me. He turned, grinning. "Better eat up and quit gabbing. When those wolves tear you apart, you won't be hungry for days."

He had the nicest way of scaring you. I could see why everyone hated him.

After dinner, it was off to the clubhouse. The videotape

session took place in a lounge there. About fifty chairs had been set up. At one end of the room was a movie screen. About ten feet in front of the screen was a big black box.

"What's that?" I asked DeVere.

"Video projector. It takes the tape and throws a picture up on the screen."

My heart sank. Back home Mike just ran our tapes on small TV monitors.

Rick laughed. He knew what I was thinking. "That's right, pal, large as life and twice as bad."

The room filled up. There were kids leaning against the window screens in the back by the time Hans Steger arrived, followed by a squad of instructors.

Steger marched to the front of the room and stood in front of the screen. "Tonight we will be analyzing Miss Nancy Ross and Mr. Buddy Berger. Lights, please."

The lights went out, the machine purred, and up on the screen Nancy Ross appeared, slightly out of focus. But she wasn't out of focus enough for anyone not to notice she had no real feeling for tennis. She didn't move instinctively. She was a coached player. You could see the money spent in every shot she made. As she played her "match" out with Mr. Steger, I waited for the comments to fly, but none did.

She sat next to me, her knees drawn up, her forehead touching them. Her eyes were closed, her neck bared to the ax about to fall.

Finally her match ended and the lights went on.

"What?" Steger asked. "No comments? I cannot believe this. Either Miss Ross is very good or she is very bad. Which is it?"

"Bad," a girl said, giving a thumbs-down sign. There was a ripple of laughter.

Rick glared at the laughers, and the laughter died.

"Perhaps someone can be more specific," Steger said.

"She didn't hustle," another girl said.

"She doesn't get her body into the ball."

"She's behind the ball."

"She—"

Rick interrupted. "I thought she did OK, Mr. Steger. She'll improve. A few weeks down here and she'll be knocking the stuffing out of the ball."

Silence. That settled it. Steger looked at Rick and then at Nancy Ross, and then at me seated on her other side. I could have sworn amusement appeared in those cold blue eyes. But maybe I was wrong.

"I agree with Mr. DeVere," he said. "Our job at Tennis World is to get Miss Ross to extend herself, lose herself in the game. Right now she is all style. A few weeks at Tennis World and I believe we will all see a definite improvement in aggressiveness and attack. Lights, please."

Nancy breathed out. She glanced up at me.

"Congratulations," I whispered.

She smiled in the darkness.

"You did fine," Rick said, on the other side.

In my innocence, I thought it all boded well for me.

My warm-up with Hans Steger appeared on the screen with me furious, slamming everything in sight right at him. It was embarrassing for me to look at my face so grim like that. I actually looked like my mother for the first time in my life.

But when the match finally started, I looked more like me, and it was also easier for me to watch. In fact, I hate to admit this, it was kind of enjoyable. I hit well and through the ball, moved OK. I was on top of every shot. I was really beginning to relax in my seat when the comments began to fly:

96

"He's lazy, Mr. Steger."

"He keeps hitting them back to the middle."

"And shallow."

"He hits a soft ball."

"Berger's slow."

"No hustle there."

"He should have hit a drop shot there. You were back on the base line."

"He had a forehand down the line there and didn't take it."

"Very slow."

I couldn't believe what I was hearing. There I was being nice to the old man, letting him teach me, and now I was catching hell for it.

"He took that backhand out of position."

"He's leaning backward."

"You can read his drop shot."

"What drop shot? He mishit that."

"He drops his racket head, Mr. Steger."

"His serve is too easy for a guy his height."

"He doesn't throw the ball up high enough."

"He's slow coming in."

"Definitely not quick. Needs to work on quickness."

And on it went. Sticking pins in the donkey. I felt myself turning red. My heart was banging away. Nancy Ross whispered: "It'll be over soon."

But it wouldn't be over soon because I had deliberately stretched the match out. I was running a gauntlet now, and they kept up their rapid-fire criticisms. No one said a good thing.

Finally it ended and as the lights went on, a voice in the back said: "He had a good warm-up anyway."

Laughter.

Mr. Steger's hard blue eyes rested on me. "Reactions, Mr. Berger?"

"Maybe I'm out of my class here. I'd sure like to see how some other guy does it."

That got a laugh. I hadn't meant it to be funny. It wasn't funny. Mr. Steger took it seriously.

"This is not a bad idea. Tom, would you get me Mr. DeVere's tape from last year? While Mr. Farrell is getting the tape, let me make a comment or two on Mr. Berger's play. Contrary to what I have just heard, I think Mr. Berger has an excellent game. He hits well. He is very fluid and for someone his size, he moves nicely. At fifteen, to be almost six feet tall usually means knee problems. He doesn't have any. However, there are negatives. Once the match started, he let up. He hit shallow, as some of you pointed out. He hit off the ball. Why? In the warm-up, I felt we were looking at a champion. In the match, no! Perhaps viewing Mr. DeVere's tape will be instructive. Not only for Mr. Berger, but for all of you. Is it ready, Tom?"

"Yes, sir."

"Lights, please."

DeVere's tape of a year ago projected onto the screen. He looked a little younger and scrawnier, but it was definitely the same person. And I could see right away what Hans Steger was up to. In their warm-up, Rick smashed ball after ball at him, just as I had done, and just as I had looked, Rick looked furious.

But there our similarity ended. For once his "match" started, Rick didn't stop looking angry. He went right on slamming the ball, only not *at* the old man, but away from him, making him run, ticking off lines, hitting corners. He hit twisting serves that bounced away from Mr. Steger. And with Mr. Steger at the base line, he dropped little drop shots at which Steger could only wave his racket. It was savage, mean, and fast. It had taken me twenty minutes to beat Hans Steger, 3–0. Rick got the job done in ten.

The lights went on.

"Comments, please?"

There were none, of course. You don't comment on a hurricane. You're just happy not to have been blown away yourself.

Finally Steger spoke. "The will to win," he said, "is more important than winning. Because it establishes a winning pattern over a lifetime of competitive tennis."

He looked around to make sure everyone understood him.

"The hunger, the passion, must be within you, no matter who your opponent is. Rick DeVere is ranked number one in sixteen-and-under this year. Tonight you saw why. He has a killer instinct that cannot be taught. He was born to win and to win the only way possible: going all out every second you're on the court."

He waited. The silence was heavy. The room was hot, but no one felt it. You could almost hear fifty hearts collectively beating. Overhead a fan whirred, the only sound in the room.

Hans Steger cleared his throat. "Perhaps you think Mr. DeVere could have beaten me as effectively by not going all out, by not hitting hard, by not trying to destroy me. No. He couldn't have. If you have eight cylinders in your tennis engine and you use only four, then you are a four-cylinder engine, and soon you will not be able to call on the other four. An English general once said that if you want to do a very good job cracking a walnut, use a sledgehammer. I agree."

"Then there's nothing left to eat," a familiar voice whispered.

99

Steger heard it too. "Mr. Norton. Do you have something to say to us all?"

"No, sir," Oliver Norton said.

"Perhaps we can all profit by your comments, Mr. Norton."

"No, sir. I don't think so, sir."

"Please stand up, Mr. Norton."

Oliver got up slowly.

"Do you know what is wrong with you as a tennis player, Mr. Norton?"

"Yes, sir. I don't have the will to win."

"And no backhand either," someone cracked. And that brought a wave of laughter. And, I thought, a certain relief. No one really likes seeing someone torn apart in front of everyone.

Hans Steger accepted it. He nodded and Oliver quickly sat down.

"In the case of certain players," Mr. Steger said, "the lack of a will to win is no great loss. But in the case of that young player who is truly talented, not to have the will to win is a real tragedy. Every once in a while we here at Tennis World welcome a player of uncommon talents. Talents that you are born with: coordination, body strength, good eyes, good wrists, good legs. Last year we welcomed Rick DeVere and watched his improvement in winter school and in the national boys' tournaments. Tonight, we welcome another young player—Buddy Berger. Buddy Berger, who came on the court today and tried to destroy me in the warm-up. Who attacked without mercy and gladdened my heart. But once the match began, he folded his tent. Perhaps he felt sorry for an old man. If he did so, he was mistaken. Pity has no place in tennis. Love is only a score.

"What fired Mr. Berger for the warm-up, however, can fire him again. And so, Mr. Berger, I say I have not lost hope for you. I know what you can do when aroused. The trick now is to help you arouse yourself . . . arouse yourself over and over, eight hours a day, seven days a week, fifty-two weeks a year. That is difficult. More than difficult, it is painful. But it is also what separates the merely good from the great, the club players from those whose pictures hang on the walls of Tennis World.

"You have your Monday schedules. Lights out in forty-five minutes. Good night."

He left the room as abruptly as he had entered, and his instructors fell in behind him.

When they had all gone, the atmosphere changed immediately.

THIRTEEN "Boy, the old man was in really good

form tonight. Berger, we owe it all to you."

"Yeah. You saw him at his best."

"Don't take that stuff we said too seriously. You're a pretty good player. You'll give DeVere a battle for camp honors."

They had come around me—the kids in our age group, boys and girls—laughing, talking, jabbing the air with their fingers. I couldn't get over their phoniness. One second these very same kids were stabbing me in the back, and the next, they were telling me what a fine fellow I was.

Carmody clapped his hands for silence. "Hold it, everyone. We owe Berger a party for that grilling, don't we?"

"For sure."

"Where?"

"Who'll get the beer?"

"Muldoon will. Who else?"

Beer? I couldn't believe I was hearing what I was hearing.

Tennis World? Where everyone lived, breathed, trained for tennis?

"Rick, can you get Muldoon to go into town for us?"

"Sure, pal. But I need up-front money."

"There's about twelve of us," Oliver Norton said, looking mostly at Nancy Ross. "A dollar apiece ought to do fine."

"Do fine for what, Norton?"

Oliver blushed. "I'm not sure. I'll think of something."

"Twelve dollars' worth is a lot of beer. Do the girls have to pay too?" a girl asked.

"A case costs ten bucks," DeVere said. "Everyone pays except Berger. Berger's the guest of honor."

"What about her?" a guy said, nodding to Nancy Ross.

Rick winked at him. "I'll pay for her." He started to put his arm around Nancy. She slid out expertly. "Thanks, but this little girl from California is going to bed early. She's had a big day."

And then before anyone could stop her, she walked out of the room. Carmody laughed. Rick DeVere looked furious. "Hell's bells," he said, "she can't do that to me." And he went out after her.

"True love if I've ever seen it," said one guy.

"What DeVere wants DeVere gets," another kid said.

"He's got absolutely no manners," Oliver said. "Someone ought to go protect her."

"How about you, Norton?"

"I don't see why Rick likes her," a girl pouted. "She's not that pretty, and she can't play at all."

"He'll teach her. DeVere likes girls who don't know anything. Well, where's the party going to be, Carmody?"

"His place," Carmody said, pointing to me.

"Berger's cottage?"

"Right. Where else? His roomies are up in Atlanta. It's the right place."

"You got a stereo, Berger?"

"He wouldn't bring a stereo down for one week. Dunn's got one in the closet though. You can get it out, Berger. Kornfeld, bring your Bee Gee's record."

"What time?"

"Half hour after lights out. Do you girls know Berger's cottage?"

"Ellsworth Vines House?"

"Right."

"We had a party there the first week of camp."

"This'll be a better one. This will be a party to end all parties."

"How do you know, Carmody?"

"I got that certain feeling, man," Carmody said. "If you know what I mean."

I didn't know what he meant.

Walking back to the cottages with Norton and Carmody, I asked them how they could possibly have parties here after lights were out.

"Simple," said Carmody, "the old man goes to bed. We pull down the shades, light up candles, and have a party."

"What about the noise?"

"He never hears it."

"What about the instructors?"

"They don't care as long as we don't wake the old man. Besides, half the time they're partying too. You can't get through this place without partying."

"He sure talked a different story to my mother back home."

"It wasn't different, Berger," Carmody said. "The old man really believes the stuff he feeds our folks. He just doesn't know what's going on here half the time."

"Do you guys really drink beer?"

"I didn't before I got down here," Norton said.

Carmody laughed. We walked by the tennis courts. They lay gleaming in the starlight, sleek and symmetrical. I wondered what my mother would think of this place if she knew the differences between night and day down here. She probably wouldn't believe it.

"See you in a while," Norton said.

"Pull the shades," Carmody said.

The lights-out signal was a record of taps played over a speaker. Just like an old World War II movie. Well, it fit.

I obediently turned off the lights and sat in the dark feeling foolish. A few minutes went by, and then I heard footsteps come quietly up the steps to my cottage and then a knock on the door.

"Open up," said Norton.

I opened the door. Oliver was carrying some records. Behind him was Carmody, holding a flashlight and a paper bag.

"Shut it right away," Carmody ordered. "And pull the darn shades. I told you to do that."

After I pulled down the shades, Carmody turned the flashlight back on. "Where's the stereo?"

"It's in the closet," Norton said. "Berger, can't you do anything?"

"I forgot."

"Maybe you don't like to dance," Norton said, "but I do."

"Let me get these candles lit first," Carmody said. He took some candles out of the bag and put them in little holders around the room. They were pretty organized. It obviously wasn't the first party given by Carmody and Norton.

Oliver was busy putting the speakers on either side of the room. He was pulling wires this way and that.

104

"We can't play the records too loud," he said. "It's not like at home."

"Berger, give me a hand with the beds."

"What for?"

"We're going to set up a dance floor. You can't dance on beds, or is that how you do it in Michigan?"

"How do the speakers look, Carmody?"

"Hmmm . . . move that one over a bit. Right. OK, just shove the beds together at that end, Berger. Here come the reinforcements. Buddy boy, be a good lad and let them in, won't you?"

I opened the door. Four boys came in carrying bags of food. Potato chips, pretzels, crackers. Beyond them I thought I could make out some more dark shapes hurrying quietly along the path toward the cottage. And I could hear some giggling. The girls were arriving.

A few minutes later the party was almost in full swing. Then there was a rap on the door and Danny Muldoon came in carrying a case of beer. "Where's Ricker?" he asked.

"He'll be along," Carmody said. "Didn't you get paid?"

"Not enough. Ah'm a buck short."

"Boy, the price of beer must've gone up."

" 'n the price of gas," Muldoon complained.

"Complain to DeVere," Norton said. "He hired you."

"Ah will. Ricker looks after me."

"Drink up, Berger," Carmody said, tossing me a can of beer. Aside from tasting beer once in a while at the table back home, I never had drunk a can of beer in my life. Other kids back in Arborville did. It was no big thing. I just never had and never wanted to. I didn't like the taste of beer.

"C'mon, Berger, it's your party. Get loose, man."

"Turn the music up, Norton."

"It's loud enough."

"Berger, have you met everyone at your party?"

"No."

"This is Chuck Walls from Ohio."

"Hi."

"Hi. You got a nice game."

"The lady with him is Fifi La Femme from Paris, France."

The girl smiled. "I'm Drew Evans from Tennessee."

"This bum is Harry de Kornfeld from New York City."

"Just Kornfeld will do, Carmody."

"Kornfeld's folks put ten grand a year into his tennis."

"What a waste."

"And this is Ann Goldstein, also from New York." She was the tall girl Carmody had been with at dinner.

"Long Island, thanks."

"Sharon Fields. She's from Boston."

"Hello, Buddy. You've got a good game."

"Thanks."

"Peggy Dietz, who, next to DeVere, is the hottest player in town."

"Just what do you mean by hottest?" Norton asked.

Everyone laughed.

"Bob Warner. Big service. Got to watch out for him."

"Kelly Mason, no serve at all."

"Nuts to you, Carmody."

"Tim Bledsoe. Tina Franks . . . and that's the lot."

I was shaking a lot of hands. The faces were already familiar from the "think" session. Kelly Mason and Chuck Walls had been particularly nasty at the "think" session. Now they were particularly friendly.

"Where's Ross?" Oliver said.

"Where's DeVere?" Kornfeld replied pointedly.

"What do you guys like so much about her?" a girl asked.

"It's not her forehand," Mason said, with a grin.

"Or her backhand either," Walls said.

"I don't think she's got *anything*," the girl said. "Let's dance."

Norton put down an empty can. "I like to see DeVere dance," he said. "Cause he dances so badly."

"DeVere, DeVere, DeVere, can't you guys stop talking about him?"

"That's where you ought to challenge him, Norton. On the dance floor. You could go on and win the Grand Slam of Dance."

"You think DeVere's that good, Chuck?" And suddenly they were talking tennis again.

"Yeah. I do. I really do."

"I think he'll be burned out by the time he's eighteen," Mason said.

"That's what they said about Connors."

"Connors never came to Tennis World. Did he, Muldoon?"

Danny Muldoon had two empty cans by his side. He was working on his third.

"Who?" he asked.

"Leave him out of it."

"Well, I still say DeVere will make it. He's a freak."

"We're all freaks, Walls," Carmody said. "This whole place is full of tennis freaks. Anyone who wants to play tennis full time has got to be a freak."

"Boy, you haven't even drunk one can, Carmody."

"I don't have to."

"Are we just going to sit here and be stupid and talk about tennis? I'm sick of tennis. Who'll dance with me?"

"Sit down, Sharon. You look better sitting down."

"Buddy, they're not gentlemen. But you are. Will you dance with me? You're the guest of honor. *You* have to be nice."

"Berger hasn't even started his beer yet. C'mon, Berger, drink up."

"Pull the tab for him, Walls."

"There. Now drink up, man."

"I don't drink beer."

"You're kidding."

"No."

Carmody grinned. "Don't you guys know? Berger's our pure knight come out of the west to slay the wicked dragon DeVere?"

"Somebody ought to write a story about this place someday."

"No one would believe it."

"Hey, where is the wicked dragon anyway?"

"Making out with Ross."

"Somebody ought to teach him a lesson," Oliver said.

"It won't be one of us."

"I think you guys are really bores. Come on, Ann, let's dance. Maybe they'll get a hint when they see two girls dancing."

"Shsh. I hear something outside."

"I do too."

"It wouldn't be any of the instructors. Take a peek, Carmody."

"Someone block the candle."

"Everyone shut up."

"What's out there, Carmody?"

"Hmmm . . . ."

"Come on. What is it?"

"Someone's coming this way carrying an alligator."

"You're drunk."

"There are no alligators around here."

"According to Tom Farrell they put one in the pond once."

"Well, it's not there now."

"Let's see that alligator."

"Stand back," Carmody said, peering around the shade. "The alligator is being carried to this cottage. It's now being carried up the steps. Someone is bringing an alligator to our party!"

Sharon Fields gave a little shriek and jumped onto the bed.

"Open the door, Kornfeld," Carmody said.

Kornfeld opened the door and in came Rick DeVere carrying a squirming, twisting, protesting Nancy Ross. She was in her pajamas. He dropped her on a bed.

"Well, I got her here."

There was absolute silence. We couldn't really believe what we were looking at. Then Walls said: "DeVere, are you nuts?"

"Naw. Just tired. Gimme a brew, Danny."

"Ah'm short a buck, Ricker," Muldoon said, tossing him a can.

"You need more than a beer," Carmody said slowly. Nancy Ross lay, small and humiliated, on the bed. We forced ourselves not to look at her. "You need a goddam spanking."

"Who's gonna give it to me? You, Carmody?"

Carmody didn't answer. DeVere eyed every other boy in the room. Norton looked away too. Finally Rick looked at me and grinned. "Here's to our guest of honor. Cheers, pal."

He drank—alone.

"Turn the music back on," someone said.

"Someone better take her home first," Kornfeld said.

I got up and went to my closet and got out my bathrobe.

"No one's taking her home," Rick said amiably. "This is her party too. You play the old man, you get chewed out, you get a party. Right?"

109

"Not if you don't want it, Rick," Sharon Fields said.

"Put this on," I said to her.

She put on the robe, not looking at me, not looking at anyone. It was embarrassing for everyone but Rick DeVere.

"If none of you boys will," Sharon said, "I'll take her home."

"I'll go with you," Drew Evans said.

"That shoots the party," Mason said.

"Come on," I said to her. "Let's go."

"Sit down, Berger," Rick said. "She's not going anywhere."

He moved over so that now he stood between us and the door.

"Don't act like an ass, DeVere," Kornfeld said.

"I went to a lot of trouble to bring her," Rick said. "She's staying for a while."

"Do you want to stay, Ross?" Sharon Fields asked.

"No," Nancy's voice was tiny, scared.

"You heard her, DeVere," Oliver said.

"No way," Rick said. He took a long drink of beer and glared at us.

"Let's not have any fights, boys," Drew Evans said.

"What's wrong with fights?" Danny Muldoon said. "My money's on Ricker."

Rick grinned at me. "I catch your act, Berger. You want to be alone with her. She's in her pajamas. Half the battle's over. You're nuts if you think I'm going to let you take advantage of that poor kid."

Danny Muldoon laughed at how Rick had turned things around.

But everyone else was looking at me, waiting to see how I would handle this. The truth was: I didn't know. He was blocking our way to the door. I'd have to knock him down to get there. I'm no fighter. I was bigger than DeVere, but I had the feeling he really liked fighting. I didn't.

"C'mon, DeVere, let them out," Mason said.

"Yeah, man," said Walls, "let's get on with the beer."

Rick ignored them. He waited for me to make my move.

Well, there was another way to the door. It meant doubling back, tiptoeing between the girls seated on the floor, climbing over some beds. It was awkward, but it could be done.

"We'll go this way," I said to Ross.

We doubled back. As I stepped carefully between Drew Evans and Ann Goldstein, who were seated cross-legged on the floor, Rick leaned over and gave me a little shove with one hand. I was off-balance anyway. I fell on top of Drew Evans.

"Hey, look at the sex fiend," Rick laughed. "You still want to go out into the dark with him, Ross?"

I felt my face redden. "Sorry," I said to her. I got up slowly. I heard people moving out of the way, clearing a space between us. There was no other way now. I walked over to Rick. He stood there on the balls of his feet, the athlete, sure of himself. Sure of me too. Sure he could handle me. He was Number 1. He ruled the roost. He was so tough, so cool, so cocky.

I hit him. I hit him as hard as I could. I hit the cool face of winning tennis. I hit the toughness and the arrogance. I hit the pride and the pain and the sweat. I hit the hunger and the desire and the will. I hit the "will" over and over. I hit it until I realized it wasn't there to be hit any more.

Rick was lying on the floor, bleeding from his nose. He had hit me too, but I hadn't felt a thing.

"Easy, man," someone said, "you damn near killed him."

A girl started to cry.

I began to shake. I wanted to cry too. Or to laugh. I wasn't sure. I just stood there. I turned to them. They were looking at me: alarmed, as though I'd gone mad.

111

"I'm sorry," I said. "I'm really sorry."

"Don't be sorry, man," Carmody said softly, "you've finally slain the dragon."

"Here comes Steger!" someone at the window said.

Everyone ran out immediately. Everyone except me and Nancy Ross and Rick DeVere, who was still lying on the floor.

FOURTEEN My memory of what happened next

is not too clear. I know that Hans Steger came in in *his* bathrobe and stared at us. Rick was sitting up holding a handkerchief to his nose.

Tom Farrell was there too, and there were others. I don't remember how many. There were beer cans all over the floor.

I don't know how long Mr. Steger stood there looking at everything. I don't remember that he even said anything. But after a while someone helped DeVere to his feet, and then they took him out. Someone else took Nancy Ross back to her cottage. Mr. Steger left with them. He hadn't said one word to me.

I cleaned up. It took me a long while because there was a lot of mess. I pushed the beds back to where they belonged and straightened out my roommates' desks. Then I packed up the stereo. When I was done I went into the bathroom to wash up. I saw for the first time that I had a puffy eye. It would be black in the morning. I could have sworn he hadn't hit me once.

Sleep was impossible. What would Steger say to me tomorrow? I'd pretend I was disappointed when he kicked me out. Returning to Michigan with a black eye. Mom would be sore. What a waste of money! He wouldn't refund the tuition. How long had I been here? Not quite a whole day. It felt like a lifetime.

There was a knock on my door. At first I thought I was dreaming it. Then the knock came again. Probably Carmody and Norton.

"Who's there?"

"Tom Farrell, Buddy."

"Come in."

Tom Farrell came in, shining a flashlight on me.

"Sorry to bug you, kid, but he wants to see you."

"Now?"

'Yes, now."

"What about?"

He laughed. "I'll give you two guesses. Get your robe on."

"I don't have it. Nancy Ross has it."

He laughed again. "Kid, you beat everything. You've turned this place upside down. Not to mention banging DeVere up pretty good."

"I'll put on my jacket. Is that OK?"

"That's fine. Do you have slippers?"

"No. Will sneakers be all right?"

"They'll do. What the well-dressed tennis player will wear. Sneakers, pajamas, and a sport jacket." Tom Farrell thought it was funny. I knew Hans Steger wouldn't.

"I'll get your robe back from her tonight."

"Why tonight?"

"She's going home in the morning."

"She didn't do anything."

"No? What was she doing here in her pajamas?"

"DeVere dragged her here. And he wouldn't let me take her back."

"That's not the story Muldoon told us."

"It's the truth."

"Tell *him*."

"I will."

We parted at the clubhouse. Tom went off toward the girls' cottages. I climbed the clubhouse steps feeling like an idiot in my sneakers, pajamas, and jacket.

Hans Steger sat behind his desk. In front of it was DeVere. Rick had two Band-Aids on his face. His eyes were puffed half-closed. His nose looked funny too. He looked at me and then looked away. The old arrogance was gone. And so was the grin too.

"Sit down," Mr. Steger said to me.

I sat down. He looked at a piece of paper in front of him. Outside the moths beat their tattoos against the window screens. Overhead another wood propeller fan turned slowly, reluctantly, having been wakened from its sleep.

"In the thirty years that Tennis World has been in existence," Steger began, "nothing like tonight has ever occurred. You came here to learn to become world class tennis players and to live in a world of ladies and gentlemen. What had we tonight? Drunkenness, brawling, a girl in her pajamas."

He stood up. Behind him was a picture of an old-time player. He looked at the picture and then turned to us.

"Aggressiveness in tennis players is desirable, necessary. Tilden had it. So did LaCoste, Vines, Perry, Kramer, Hoad, Connors. But their arena was the court, not the cottage. If you two children want to fight, fight on the courts with your rackets!"

He sat down and picked up the piece of paper.

"Tomorrow at three P.M. instead of the usual round robin, you two will have your really important battle on Court One."

My heart sank. I wasn't being sent home.

Rick said: "I can't see too good, sir."

"You'll see better by tomorrow, Mr. DeVere," Steger snapped.

114

"Yes, sir."

"You are excused, Mr. DeVere."

"Yes, sir. Thank you, sir."

Mr. Steger waited till the screen door clicked shut behind Rick.

"Mr. Berger, you came within a hair of doing permanent damage to one of the finest young tennis players in the world."

"I didn't mean to, Mr. Steger. He started it."

"Not according to what I heard. According to what I heard you walked up to him and hit him first."

"Yes, sir, that's true. But he wouldn't let me take Ross back to her cottage."

"Of course he wouldn't. Boys are forbidden to be in girls' cottages and vice versa. Mr. DeVere was only doing what was correct."

My God, I thought, he has it all turned around.

"Can I tell my side of it, sir?"

"You have no side, Mr. Berger. It is only with great difficulty that I will be able to prevent Mr. DeVere's family from bringing criminal charges against you. At least five people present said you went on hitting him after he was hurt. There was no stopping you, they said. They said you looked as though you wanted to kill him."

I winced.

"Mr. Berger, you were *accepted* here because of your tennis ability—not for your skill with your fists. In Arborville, it was also indicated to me that you were involved with a girl. One of the reasons your mother thought you could profit from Tennis World was that you could concentrate on your game down here. What happens? You get involved with a girl down here. Against the camp rules. My decision is that from now till the end of the week you are on probation, Mr. Berger. You are restricted to your cottage after dinner.

115

However . . . ," he paused and leaned forward," you can make up for your bad social behavior by your play on the courts."

He looked into me. And those hard blue eyes, I swear, began to gleam.

"I want to see that same aggressiveness appear on the tennis court. If you want to kill Rick DeVere, kill him there! As good as Mr. DeVere is, you can be better, Mr. Berger. You can be the number one player in America if you want it enough. Do you *want* it, Mr. Berger?

There was absolutely nothing to say any more. He was crazy. The biggest tennis freak of all.

Tom Farrell was waiting for me outside.

"How'd it go?" he asked.

"I'm playing DeVere at three o'clock tomorrow. He didn't kick me out."

"You're too good a player to be kicked out," Tom said. "She wasn't. Here."

He tossed my bathrobe at me.

"She said to say good-by to you, kid. And thanked you."

"I tried to tell him. He wouldn't let me."

Tom smiled. "It doesn't make any difference, does it?"

I didn't understand that.

"He's running a tennis camp. Tennis is what this place is about. That's all that's important. Good night, kid."

"Good night, Tom."

I walked slowly back to Ellsworth Vines House. It took me a long time to fall asleep.

fifTEEN
In the morning I had a black eye. Rick DeVere had two. The story of the party was all over Tennis World. I expected to be condemned. Instead, kids came up,

touched my arm, and let me know they were glad someone had finally done something about Rick DeVere.

They told me they'd be rooting for me that afternoon.

No one mentioned Nancy Ross. It was as though she had never existed.

"Unfair," said Oliver at lunch. "This whole place is built on unfairness. You've got to go out and finish the job on that louse, Berger."

"Can you see OK?" Carmody asked.

"Fine," I said.

"Look at DeVere. He looks like a panda. I bet he can't see a thing."

"He's ripe to be taken on the court too, Buddy," Carmody said.

"I'll do my best," I said, but the butterflies were starting to fly in my belly.

It was beginning to dawn on me that in a few hours I would be stepping onto the same court with the number one sixteen-and-under player in the United States. How do you get ready for something like that?

You don't. The more you think about something like that, the worse your stomach gets.

That morning I had instruction from Tom Farrell. He worked on my game with an eye toward my match with Rick. He told me to change pace on him. Don't just top-spin him. Don't fall into a groove or he'd slaughter me. Slice a few, mix them up, drop shots, lobs, don't let him get into his groove because his groove would kill my groove.

This was the summer for that kind of advice. The summer I was constantly playing people better than me, trying to foul up their game rather than beat them with my own. The awful part was: It worked. The junk I fed to Rob Parker he couldn't digest; the moon balls I popped drove Mr. Hankins out of his mind. Maybe it was the only way I could win.

At 3:00 P.M. a huge crowd was at Court Number 1. Not only our age group, but other age groups too. The word was out. It was a different crowd than the one that had come to watch my "match" with Mr. Steger. This crowd was quiet, expectant. The butterflies were careening around inside me now. And they were talking to me too. "He's number one," they kept saying. "Don't make a fool of yourself. Stay in the game. . . ."

Rick kept me waiting. Unnecessary psych. But then when he finally appeared, I calmed down. I calmed down because he came onto the court with two black eyes and a puffy nose. Laughter went up. Rick scowled, but it didn't stop the laughter. His days as ruling dragon—at least off the court—were over. It even made him look a little human. I relaxed.

If Rick had a vision problem with those eyes, he didn't show it in the warm-up. The balls he hit, with a minimum of effort, came zinging back to within inches of the base line. Heavy balls too. Trouble, I thought. Trouble.

He didn't talk to me. I didn't talk to him.

A few minutes after 3:00 P.M. Hans Steger climbed into the umpire's chair and stopped our warm-up.

"This match," he announced, "will be two out of three sets. The players will make their own calls. There will be no appeal. To my left is Mr. Buddy Berger from Arborville, Michigan. To my right is Mr. Rick DeVere from Dallas, Texas. I will flip a coin for choice of service. Mr. DeVere, will you call it, please?"

"Heads."

"It is heads."

"I'll serve."

"This side's fine with me," I said.

"Let play begin."

Play began in a hurry. Rick aced me on his first serve. I

118

wasn't even close to getting a racket on it. He hadn't practiced a serve that hard.

I got my racket on his next serve, and immediately he began driving me all over the court. He hit harder than I did. He put more of his body into shots than I did. In fact, he put all of his body into them. I looked a little better maybe, but he was, like my mother, all graceless, relentless attack.

He drove cross-court. I threw myself at a ball skidding away from me and looped it up. It caught the line behind him. Applause. There had been no applause for his ace. The crowd was with me.

"Fifteen all."

He tried for an ace again. My return was weak. Up at the net, quick as a cat, he put it away.

"Thirty–fifteen," intoned Mr. Steger.

"Come on, Berger," someone shouted.

The next point went on forever, it seemed, with me running all over the court retrieving. For some reason he was content to stay in his backcourt and just run me with those hard topspin drives. I kept getting to the ball and hitting it back to the middle, hoping he'd hit one out or at least hit one shallow enough to let me get back into the game. But he didn't. He just kept banging away at the corners until I finally didn't get to one.

"Forty–fifteen."

I returned his serve down the middle. He smacked to my backhand and came to the net. I hit it as hard as I could, trying to pass him cross-court. It got by him. I couldn't tell whether it was in or out. He signaled "fair ball" with his left hand. Applause. But what impressed me was that he could be so honest in his calls. Off the court he was a louse. On the court he was professional. In Arborville, lots of junior players

119

saw balls "out" that they wanted to be out. He could have "seen" this one out.

At 40–30 he bounced the ball several times before serving. I swayed, trying to stay loose and mindless. But my mind clicked away. He'll blast it. No, he'll hit a twist to my backhand. He'll— He blasted it right at me. I was asleep. I jumped aside. (Too slow!) My return was a soft chip. He banged it away for the game point.

Just the same, I liked to think it had gone longer than he expected, this first game. But it was hard to know what he thought. His expression didn't change. Once again, he reminded me of my mother.

I won my service because he lay back and let me come to the net. He also missed two passing shots. Rob Parker wouldn't have missed them, but Rob didn't try for winners the way Rick did. Just the same, I didn't feel out of my class.

We each held service through the first seven games. And then with the score 3–4 and me serving, he took over. He took over very simply by stepping up the pace. Out of nowhere, I was caught in the DeVere hurricane. Everything began happening faster. He banged my serves back harder than I hit them. He was at the net; I couldn't pass him. I couldn't get a ball over his head.

He won that game and then took his serve and that was the first set, 6–3. And I wondered why he had suddenly turned it on.

He didn't turn it off in the second set. I could hear my mother inside my skull telling me to moon-ball, junk it, slice, drop, do anything to slow up the hurricane, appease its wrath, confuse its direction.

But I decided not to. There had been enough of that already. Win or lose, I was going to play my game.

It was tough. Rick DeVere was quicker than I was, he hit harder than I did, he had a greater variety of shots, he was

120

more accurate than I was. He was just a better player. He was born a better player and he would die a better player.

I was constantly on the defensive. Constantly coping. The tide was always coming in. The wind was always blowing. This was what being out of your class meant. this was the difference between local champ and world champ.

In just seconds, it seemed, I was down, 3–0.

Some kids started to leave. As we changed sides Tom Farrell gave me new balls and told me to change my game. "Take something off it, kid," he said.

"No way, Tom."

"Why not?"

"I don't want to win that way. I can't win that way."

He shook his head. I knew what he was thinking: born loser. Maybe he was right. But at least I'd have the satisfaction of losing *my* way.

I kept on hitting and he kept hitting harder than me. The score was 4–0 . . . 5–0.

At 5–0, something happened. Perhaps *his* mind kicked on. Anyway, he let up just a little. People often do that when they're way ahead or way behind. Also he made a couple of errors. His was an all-out game. When you try for winners, you can also miss. Home-run hitters strike out more than singles hitters.

I broke his service. And then at 1–5, my serve began catching lines for aces. I had nothing to lose by trying for aces. I won that game with four straight points.

That halted the exodus of the crowd.

Rick tried to tighten his game again, but it's not easy, when you've had a walkabout, to come storming back. He should have been more patient and just hit with me a while. But he was *numero uno*, and he had to try for winners. He was now missing. Soon it was 5–3, and then 4–5. I think all the kids who had left came back. Word somehow always gets out around tennis courts. Maybe it's the applause. You can feel tension rising up from a court like heat waves. The stands were filled again.

I sat on the bench and toweled off. I was down, 4–5. If I won the next game we'd be into extra games and maybe into sixes and sevens. Nobody had said anything about a tie-breaker. It could go on a long time. He was settling down again. He'd probably start all over again and run me, as he had in the beginning. It would be more sweat and pain. And if I won this set, that would mean a long third set and another hour of pain and concentration. And if by some crazy fluke I won the third set, I'd be a shoo-in for Hans Steger's winter school. I'd be in the Junior Davis Cup groove. I'd be invited to the Easter Bowl, other national tournaments. New Orleans. Dallas.

"Mr. Berger," a voice called from the umpire's chair. A harsh old tennis voice.

Rick was waiting on the court.

Stop thinking, I told myself. Play tennis. Empty out your head. You want this. You want to win this match.

There was applause for me as I came on the court. They could see it too. They could see a new star in the tennis galaxy.

Rick served. My forearm tightened. I chipped it back. He put it away. Rick served. I tried to hit it hard, I wanted to hit it hard, but something inside held me back. Too careful, I netted the ball. Rick served, I lobbed back, trying to make an offensive lob. It was too shallow. He blasted an overhead to the corner. Rick served. I slammed his second serve five feet out.

The glorious battle that had them all holding their breaths had suddenly ended.

With a whimper.

Mine.

SIXTEEN

"Perhaps," the old man said, "just as there is a will to win, so there is a will to lose. A desire to fall short of greatness."

I looked at him across a gap of a million years.

"You had it in your hands, but you wouldn't take it. You're not a competitor, Buddy Berger. I thought as much when we met in Michigan. A true competitor is willing to die for his art. You're not willing to do that, are you?"

No, old man, I'm not.

"Rick DeVere has died a thousand times. On a thousand courts."

Let him, I thought. I want to live.

The old man looked at me with contempt. I had failed him. Outside, the night insects crashed against the window screens and the frogs croaked in the pond beyond the tennis courts.

"What did he want with you?" Carmody asked. He and Oliver were waiting for me on my porch. Everyone knew I was restricted to my cottage after dinner, or after any after-dinner tennis "think" session.

"He wanted to call me a quitter."

"The jerk," Carmody said.

"Well, he was right," Oliver said. "You did quit in that last game."

"Shut up, Norton," Carmody said.

"Why don't you go beat him for yourself, Oliver," I said.

Carmody laughed. "Absolutely correct."

"I would if I could," Oliver spluttered. "But I can't."

"If Ross had been there," Carmody asked me, "would that have made a difference?"

I shook my head. "He's better than me, Tommy. He always will be. And I don't have the stuff to go all the way. I

123

don't want it badly enough. Everything the old man said, it's true. I don't have it."

"Who has, for pete's sake?"

"DeVere," Oliver said.

"Let him keep it," Carmody said. His voice became cheerful. "Anyway, those black eyes are going to last awhile, and the memory of them will last the summer."

"That's right," Oliver said. "He won't be throwing his weight around at any more parties. That's for sure."

"You guys are still going to parties?"

"Of course," Carmody said. "You would too if you had to stay the whole summer here."

I thought he was probably right.

I should have written to Chris that night, but it's hard to write a letter when you don't feel particularly proud of yourself, and you don't particularly like where you are. I'd put it off to later in the week. Maybe things would get better as the week went along.

But they didn't. Kids were still friendly to me, at least as long as Rick still had his black eyes, but I could feel they didn't approve of my sudden death out on the tennis court.

Rick DeVere and I never exchanged another word. Which didn't bother me one bit.

Another person who stopped talking to me was Hans Steger. At first I thought maybe he hadn't quite given up on me and was trying one last way to motivate me.

I remembered Dad telling me how the Holdens—a famous tennis-coaching couple in Detroit years ago—operated. They would take the best young players in each group to tournaments around Michigan. They expected all of their pupils to reach the quarterfinals, at least. If you got bumped off in the early rounds, you were handed a bus ticket as you came off the court. Not later. As you came off the court. And not one word was spoken to you. You had to go back to Detroit alone. All of this was supposed to make you want not to lose, but Dad said it destroyed a lot of kids.

I thought of this because I was getting the same kind of treatment from Hans Steger. (In spite of the fact that my mother was paying him a lot of money to work on my game.) If Steger and I passed each other on one of the camp roads, those blue eyes looked through me as though I was invisible.

After a while I realized he wasn't trying to motivate me— he'd just written me off. It upset me until Carmody put it into perspective. "What do you care, Buddy? He's off your back."

Carmody was absolutely right. But it was still nothing to write to Chris about. The upshot was I didn't write to Chris at all that week. Or to my mother. It would be a long time before I forgave her for shipping me off to Tennis World.

I didn't want to think about her and Matt either, which I'd be doing if I wrote her. Nor did I want to think about my match with Dad coming up on Sunday, and whether I had improved enough to beat him. That didn't matter any more. None of it mattered. I had seen all the worms that lived at the bottom of the tennis can—and that "bottom" was the top too! I didn't want any part of it.

Friday, after my last lesson from Tom Farrell, Tom sat me down under a palm tree and he talked about my game. I had heard that Steger did this with every pupil before they left camp. Tom had been instructed to do it with me.

He was embarrassed, and after mumbling about one thing or another, he told me I ought to work on improving my quickness. He showed me an exercise that would help. (Though we both agreed you couldn't *teach* someone to be quick. Still, he went through the form.) After that he couldn't think of anything else.

"How about my attitude?" I teased him. "Shouldn't I be working on that?"

Tom looked embarrassed.

"Hell, kid . . . you know . . . well, it's only a game." And then we both laughed.

I thought of something real to ask him—something I had wondered about, sitting alone on the porch of Ellsworth Vines House at night.

"Tom, can you be a really good tennis player and *not* want to go all the way to the top?"

He understood what I was getting at. He was silent a moment, and then he said "No." Flatly.

"Why not?"

"Because unless you compete, you can't ever find out how good you really are. Buddy, you don't even know what *good* means until you play with the best. Good compared to whom? Good compared to Carmody? You're great compared to him. Good compared to DeVere? That you're not. Not yet. So you've got to play with Rick and with those kids in California and Australia and Sweden and Russia who're as good as Rick and getting better. You've got to get into the deep end of the pool."

"Maybe it's not worth it."

"Lots of people think that."

"Do you?"

"No, I don't."

"You mean, you think it is worth it?"

"Yes."

"Did you do it at fifteen?"

"No. But I wasn't as good as you are at fifteen."

"But you're really good now."

126

"Compared to whom, kid?" He laughed easily. "Buddy, if I was that good I'd be on tour somewhere. I'd be with the Gullicsons, McEnroe, and Fleming. But I'm not that good. So I'm down here in the old man's pressure cooker trying to take some of the heat off of you. The fact is: I'm a loser too."

And now we were both embarrassed. Why couldn't tennis conversations just be about tennis? What was there about tennis that jutted down into your soul? Why couldn't the game just be played on the courts?

That night it was farewell to Carmody and Norton, who came over after dinner to watch me pack.

"I envy you, Berger," Carmody said. "I'd be going home if my folks would let me."

"Me too," Oliver said.

"Thanks, but I won't get a great welcome at home when my mother finds out I didn't get into winter school."

"He doesn't take many."

"She knows that. But she thinks I could be the best in the world."

"Tell her you probably ought to have a career in boxing," Oliver said.

We all laughed.

"Where's the party tonight?"

"Helen Wills Moody."

"Who's she?"

"That's the name of the cottage. Sharon's giving it. No beer though. No Muldoon. And no DeVere. It ought to be OK. You want to come?"

"No, thanks. Say good-by to everyone for me. I'm leaving before breakfast."

"Right-o. Should we say good-by to Rick for you?"

127

I laughed. "Why not?"

"You know, his black eyes are practically gone," Oliver said. "I wish one of us had taken a picture of him to show any new kids coming in next week."

"Maybe one of the new kids will be able to take him on the court."

"I doubt it," Carmody said. "You came the closest. But you know, somewhere in this big country there has got to be a louse like Rick playing tennis eight hours a day wanting to be *numero uno*. Only he'll be a bigger louse than Rick and so he'll beat him."

"Could you hand me that shirt?"

"This one?"

"Yeah. I'm going to wear the other one home."

I spread the shirts around on top of my pants. My dirty tennis stuff was wrapped on the bottom in a plastic bag.

"How long's it take you to get home?" Oliver asked.

"Four hours."

"Your mom going to meet you?"

"And her boyfriend."

Carmody whistled. "Funny deal."

"I'm used to it."

"Why didn't you go live with your old man?"

"She got me in the divorce. Me and the Lincoln."

"That's better than you and a Chevy," Oliver said.

"Rambler. My dad's got the last Rambler in Michigan just about."

"My father drives a Chevy," Carmody said. "He thinks it's democratic. Hey, you get to play your old man in that tournament, don't you?"

"Sunday. The final."

"Gonna beat him?"

"Probably not."

"Didn't you learn anything down here?" Carmody asked, grinning.

"Yes, but nothing that will improve my game."

They laughed.

"Who'd you rather beat, Buddy, your father or Rick DeVere?" Oliver asked.

"DeVere," I said.

"Not me," said Oliver. "I'd rather beat my father than Rick any day, and my father doesn't even know how to play tennis."

We all laughed. It was nice sitting there with those two guys. They would leave a pleasant aftertaste of Tennis World. Not that they were really my friends. They were just stuck here too.

"Well," Carmody said, "we got to go and get ready for our party."

Getting ready for the party meant changing from their fancy eating duds to blue jeans.

"Take care, Berger," Carmody said.

"You too, Tommy."

"Beat your old man," Norton said.

"Beat your own."

"I might write you on a rainy day," Carmody said.

"I might answer you on a rainy day."

We kidded some more, knowing we'd never write and probably would never see each other again. Then they left. I finished packing and got my rackets together.

After that I washed up and sat out on the porch of Ellsworth Vines House and watched Tennis World settle down for the night.

After lights out, about twenty minutes later, I thought I saw the flickering of candles across the way. I watched for a while and sure enough, I saw the dark shapes of kids sneaking between cottages, going over to the girls' side of Tennis World.

All this while the old man slept.

Which wasn't, I thought, a bad thing to do.

"You've got tennis in your bloodstream."

—*Dr. Richard Berger to his son
Buddy after their match in the
finals of the Arborville Men's
Open*

III. Arborville

SEVENTEEN The big Delta jet flew along the Detroit River, flaps down, and over Lake St. Clair. The lake was filled with white sails. It looked as though a thousand yachts were racing across the lake toward the Canadian shore.

Then the plane banked left and we were descending over expressways, roads, ball fields, houses . . . coming closer and closer to real life. Matt and Mom would be waiting for me at Metro. The questions would come in rapid-fire from my mother: How had it gone? Had I been invited to winter school? What was Steger like as a teacher? Did he have any special tricks? What was the competition like? Who had I beaten? Had they been impressed with my game? What was the food like? The lodging? Who were some of the instructors? Had I lost to anyone?

She'd get her answers all right. She'd even get answers to questions she didn't have.

Matt Bigby wasn't there.

My mother stood by herself in the terminal, peering at the incoming passengers. I saw her before she saw me. And in a single instant I knew something had happened. She looked different, blurred almost. Maybe it was because I was seeing her before she saw me, or maybe it was just that I hadn't seen her for a week. But she looked different, younger . . . softer.

She saw me and waved. And when I came up to her, she surprised me by hugging me. My mother was not the hugging type.

"You look wonderful," she said. "What happened to your eye?"

I guess some of the bruise was left.

"Mr. Steger slugged me when I missed an overhead."

She laughed. "What really happened?"

"I'll tell you about it later. Where's Matt?"

"He . . . couldn't make it. He —" She stopped. Flustered. Then she laughed. "I'll tell *you* about it later."

"You seem in a pretty good mood."

"I'm glad you're back."

"I'm glad to be back."

We walked toward the baggage claim.

"How was the flight?"

Now the questions would start. Begin with the flight and work their way back to Tennis World. Well, I was ready. More than ready.

"The flight was fine."

"Did they serve lunch?"

"A ham sandwich and milk."

"I've made a nice tuna salad for us at home."

I looked at her. My mother? Talking about something she had cooked?

"Why?"

"I thought you'd be hungry."

"Didn't you play tennis this morning?"

She smiled. "I have a confession to make. I haven't played in two whole days."

"You're kidding."

"No."

"Are you injured?"

She laughed. "Quite the opposite. I'm . . . uh . . . fine."

And there she was again, my mother, who always moved sure-footed through emotional thickets, suddenly being clumsy.

"Let's get your suitcase."

And evasive. It wasn't like her at all.

"Don't you want to know what Tennis World was like?" I'd bring her back to reality.

136

"Of course. What was it like?"

"It was awful."

"I gathered that."

I stared at her. "How did you gather that?"

"I got a letter from Mr. Steger."

"Already?"

"It came Thursday."

Thursday? He could have written it after the party, then, even after the match with DeVere. I winced. Here it comes, I thought.

"What did he say?"

"He said Tennis World wasn't the place for you."

I waited.

"Is that all he wrote?"

"That was about it."

And it didn't seem to bother her. This was weird. Very weird.

"Did he tell you I'm *not* invited to go to winter school?"

"Yes."

"Aren't you angry?"

"No."

"Why not?"

"I'm sorry you had a bad week, Buddy, and I'm sorry I was the cause of it. Here comes your bag. Let me carry your rackets."

"No," I said, "I can carry everything." I suddenly felt angry and cheated. She was ahead of me again, anticipating everything.

"It's a long walk to the car."

"That's OK. Did he tell you about the party in my cottage?"

"No. You can read the letter for yourself when we get home."

"I will. I'll also fill you in on everything he left out. Even the things the crazy old man doesn't know about. I'm going to tell you what it's really like down there, Mom. I learned a lot down there. And you know what the biggest thing I learned was?"

"What was that, Buddy?"

"That I don't want to play competitive tennis any more."

I waited. If anything would bring the explosion, the fire and lightning, the old Mom back . . . this was it.

But all she said was: "Well, it's good you found this out now rather than later."

We walked out of the terminal. I was stunned. Something had happened up here while I was gone. I was almost afraid to ask what.

We got into the Lincoln and drove to the tollbooth. Mom gave the woman in the booth a dollar. The wooden barrier lifted, the green light blinked the words THANK YOU, and we headed for I-94 and Arborville. I waited till she got us off the ramp and onto the expressway.

"OK," I said, "I blew my chances at Tennis World and made a royal mess of things and you're not sore. Either you're faking it or it's real."

She smiled. "It's real, Buddy."

"What's real?"

She nodded. It was come-clean time for both of us. She took a deep breath. "Matt asked me to marry him, Buddy, and this time I said yes."

I should have known.

"I think we both learned a lot this week, Buddy. I went to school too. It was a different kind of school. Matt was my teacher. We had long talks every day. I didn't play much tennis this week; he didn't go to work very much. We talked our lives and hearts out, Buddy. He made me understand a lot of things about myself, and about you and me. . . ." She

138

stopped. . . . It was hard for her. She wasn't a glib person. I suddenly realized why she had met me alone at the airport. She wanted to go through it alone with me. It scared me a little. I looked out the window.

"He made me see I was using you in my war with your father. And that's wrong. I hope things will be different from now on, Buddy. I'm going to work very hard at being a better person."

Oh God, I thought. The only thing worse than her being a tyrant was her being humble.

"Matt's very fond of you, Buddy. He knows he can't replace your father. He knows how close you and your father are, and it makes him happy. He likes you and respects you and I know you're going to like and respect him too."

The flat, dull land between Detroit and Arborville flowed by. Gas stations, little white houses with green plastic swimming pools in fenced yards, tricycles. . . .

"You don't have to love Matt, Buddy, but I know you're going to like him."

"When are you getting married?"

"In late September."

"What's the big rush?"

"Why wait?"

"Do I stay with you or move to Dad's?"

A look of pain crossed her face, but then she was herself again.

"I hope you'll want to stay with us."

"I'm going to call Chris up the minute I get back."

"Of course. You should."

It was crazy. I felt like banging my head against the windshield.

"Did you line up someone for me to hit with this afternoon?"

She bit her lip. "I forgot."

And that did it! That little "I forgot" told me more than anything else that we were now living in two different worlds. After shipping me off to a place I hated, she had forgotten why.

"I'll get someone for you to hit with when we get home."

"Don't bother," I said, "I'll find someone myself."

While she set the table for the two of us, I read Hans Steger's letter.

> Dear Mrs. Berger,
>
> This is to inform you that while your son Buddy has a genuine physical talent for tennis, his mental attitude is such that I cannot admit him to winter school at Tennis World.
>
> Later you will receive from his instructor a detailed report on different aspects of his game, but his recent behavior on and off the court leads me to tell you not to have false hopes about his future in competitive tennis on anything but a club scale.
>
> Sincerely,
> Hans Steger

"Diplomatic guy," I said, and folded up the letter.

"It doesn't make any difference," she said. "We're going to live a different kind of life from now on."

"Would you like to know what he meant by my behavior *off* the court?"

"Not particularly. Would you like milk with your tuna salad?"

But I wasn't going to let her change the subject. She was going to have to pay for all this new happiness of hers.

"You remember all that stuff he fed us about boys and girls being separate at Tennis World?"

140

"Yes, I do, but none of it matters any more, Buddy. What's done is done."

"Those kids have parties practically every night. They drink beer. And some of them smoke."

"Is that right?"

"That crazy old man only runs it in the daytime. At night a lot of funny things go on. You know what really happened to my eye? I got into a fight with Rick DeVere at a party. Would you believe it? And I gave him two black eyes and a bloody nose. Would you like to hear what Steger said to me afterward?"

Mom's face turned white. "Buddy, I told you I was sorry. I was wrong to have sent you there. I've apologized. What more do you want?"

"I want you to know what a lousy, lonely time I had down there while you and Matt were having fun up here. I want you to know that Steger *liked* my fighting with DeVere. He put me on the court with him the next day and had the whole camp watch. And I quit, Mom. I quit in the middle of the match. I gave up. With everyone watching, I gave up. I'm a quitter, Mom. That's also what I learned about myself. I'm a quitter."

"Buddy, please stop. Please, please, please stop."

But I couldn't stop. I don't even remember what I said, but I wasn't even talking. I was yelling at her, accusing her, until I finally got what I wanted.

She broke into tears. She started crying. And it wasn't easy for her to cry. She was the Ice Age, frozen rock that didn't move easily.

But now she melted. She buried her face in her hands and wept.

And then I stopped. Because I was crying too. Tears were running down my face. I ran around the table and buried my face in her neck.

141

"Mom, I'm sorry. . . ."

"It's all right, Buddy. It's all right."

And I knew once again she was right.

EIGHTEEN After that I called Chris. Though it wasn't immediately after that. All week down at Tennis World I thought about Chris and started letters to her in my head and never once wrote one. And then I came home and told Mom the first thing I was going to do was call Chris, but I hadn't done that yet either.

We washed up, Mom and me, feeling kind of sheepish about the tears. And then we ate the tuna salad and talked about what had happened in Arborville the week I was gone. Nothing much.

After we ate, I called Chris. I really wanted to call from upstairs the way I usually did. I mean, even if things were different between Mom and me, a phone call is still a private thing. But I guess I had to prove something, so I called Chris from the kitchen phone, not six feet from where Mom was rinsing out dishes in the sink.

The phone rang and rang. Dad was probably at the hospital. Carol could be anywhere. But that darn Chris, she ought to be there. She knew I was coming in around noon today.

Finally the phone was picked up on the tenth or so ring. Carol—out of breath.

"Me," I said.

"Buddy, dear, you're back."

"Yeah."

"I was out in the garden. How are you? What was it like down there?"

"It was . . . OK. Is Chris there?"

Hesitation. "She's out at the club."

"Oh."

"I'm sorry your father's not here. He's dying to hear about your week."

"Is she in a tournament?"

"No. I think she's just hitting. When did you get in?"

"A little while ago. Who's she hitting with?"

More hesitation. "I'm not sure."

"I'll go out and see her."

"She ought to be home soon, Buddy."

"That's OK. I need the exercise. I'll bike out now."

"I'll run you over," Mom said.

"My mother will take me, Carol. Listen, tell Dad I didn't improve my game one bit down there."

Carol laughed. "He'll be glad to hear that because he didn't play once this week. That new Swedish doctor and his family arrived and we've *all* been working hard to get them settled."

"Good. Maybe I'll have a fighting chance tomorrow. I'll see you later, Carol."

"Buddy, by the time you get there she'll probably be home."

"That's OK. I ought to hit a ball once before tomorrow."

I hung up and turned to Mom. "Did you mean that about giving me a ride there?"

"Of course."

"Did you see Chris out there this week?"

"No. But I haven't been out there much this week."

"You've got a match tomorrow too, Mom."

Mom smiled. "Buddy, I ought to be able to beat Ruth Brady once more after all these years."

"Careful now . . . overconfidence can destroy concentration."

143

She laughed. "Go up and change and I'll run you out."

Mom drove me to the far edge of the parking lot at the club. From there you can see practically all the courts. Chris was at the far end. I couldn't see who she was hitting with. Probably Janet Sklar by the velocity of the balls coming back at her. Chris looked pretty good herself. She was reaching better with that two-handed backhand.

"Buddy, Matt's coming over tonight. We'll be eating at six-thirty."

"I'll be back by then, Mom. And thanks."

She smiled, and drove off. It was the world turned upside down. Mom driving me to see Chris.

"Hello, Buddy Berger," a voice called down from the club-house deck.

"Oh, hello, Mr. Thurston." Cliff Thurston was the club manager.

"I thought you were down in Florida."

"I was. I just got back."

"What was it like?"

"Interesting, Mr. Thurston."

"You think you learned enough to beat your old man tomorrow?"

"I doubt it."

He laughed and waved me along.

"Berger!" Joel Cohen called out from Court 3, where he and Tom Hannigan were hitting.

"Hello, you guys."

"What's the deal, man? When'd you get back?"

"Just now. You want to hit with me later?"

"Which one of us?"

"Either."

"I will," Joel said quickly.

144

"Methinks I hear a familiar voice," Paul Cotter said. He strolled out onto the clubhouse deck holding a Coke. "When did you get back, star?"

"A little while ago."

"Well, let's hear about it."

"Later. I want to see Chris."

"She's uh . . . hitting with someone, Buddy."

"I see that, Cotter, but she'll make time for me."

I walked behind the windscreen to the end court. It would be a real surprise for Chris when I popped onto the court.

It was. Not only for Chris, but for me. There was Chris all right, across the net. Only she wasn't hitting with Janet Sklar or with any girl. She was hitting with a guy. A tall, blond guy I'd never seen before.

I just stood there and watched them whack the ball back and forth. He could hit too. Then Chris saw me. Her eyes widened. But the ball came zipping over to her at that instant, and she concentrated on it and hit it back.

"Buddy," she called out, without taking her eye off the game, "I'll be right there."

But their rally went on and on until she finally hit one into the net.

Then she came up to the net—not around it, not around the court toward me, the way I started over to her, but up to the center of the net, so she could pick up the ball and say hello to me at the same time.

I had to go onto the court to be with her. Not the last word in tennis etiquette, but that's what I did.

The big blond guy protested. "Please," he said.

He had a foreign accent. Chris and I met at the net. I wanted to reach over and kiss her. But there was the net and she was tapping up the ball with her racket.

"Buddy, when did you get in?"

I couldn't believe it.

"A little while ago," I heard my voice answer calmly.

"I'd like you to meet Eric Nielsen from Sweden. You remember Dad telling us about the Swedish family coming over?"

I turned to the guy. He was seventeen or eighteen. He smiled at me with twice as many teeth as human beings are supposed to have.

"Eric, this is Buddy."

"Of course," the guy said, beaming, "Chris tells me about you. You were down at Tennis World."

He stuck out his hand. I didn't want to shake it, but I did.

"Eric's been to Tennis World too, Buddy."

"Yust to visit. Last summer," he said, flashing all those extra teeth at me. "I play with some top people there. You know Vic Morgan?"

I shook my head.

"Tim Rutherford?"

I shook my head again. Back in Tennis World. Do you know . . . do you know?

"They're eighteen-and-unders, Eric," Chris said. "Buddy's only fifteen."

Only fifteen? How old did she think she was, for pete's sake?

"Oh, yes, of course," he beamed. "But you are big for your age. I hear you are number one around here."

I shook my head. I didn't quite trust myself to talk.

"Go ahead and hit some, you two," Chris said. "Buddy needs the practice. He's got a big match tomorrow. This might make you feel better, Buddy. Dad hasn't played once this week."

"Dad." Not "*your* dad" any more. One week, and now my dad was her dad.

146

"You want to hit some, Buddy?" Eric Nielsen asked.

No, I didn't want to hit some with the creep. I'd come fifteen hundred miles to see my girl, to kiss her, hold her hand, go off somewhere and be alone, and here she was telling me to hit tennis balls with a Swedish jockstrap. A wave of anger flooded me.

"Sure I'll hit some," I said, "but first . . . how are you, Chris?"

She got the message. She blushed. "I'm fine."

But she wasn't. She was embarrassed. Boy, had things ever gotten turned around! My mother had been embarrassed because she felt free to hug and kiss me. Chris was embarrassed because she didn't.

"These balls are pretty good," Nielsen said. He bounced one to show me.

"Swell," I said, "let's go."

Once more I was back in Tennis World. Only this time it wasn't Rick DeVere across the net, but a Swedish guy. And the prize wasn't a scared kid named Nancy Ross, but Chris.

Nielsen put a ball into play, nice and soft. I slammed it to his feet at a hundred miles an hour. He looked puzzled. He put another one into play. I slammed it at him again. This time he frowned. He put the third one into play. I slammed it. He was ready and chopped it back. I came in and took it waist high and slammed it into the corner. It caught the line. I had never hit three balls harder or more accurately in my life. Not even against Hans Steger in the warm-up down there. I was probably the world's best warm-up hitter.

Nielsen stared at Chris. He didn't understand.

I walked off the court. "That's enough. This is stupid. I just came out here to say hello to you, Chris. I don't feel like playing at all. I've had enough tennis. I'll see you later, Chris."

147

"Buddy, don't."

"Don't what?"

"Don't act like an idiot."

"I'm not acting like one. I am one."

As I walked away from them, I heard Eric say: "I do not understand. Is it something I have done?"

I didn't hear what Chris replied, if anything.

Joel Cohen saw me going by again.

"C'mon, Buddy."

"Can't. I've got to go home."

"You just got here, man."

"I know. But I've got to get back."

I saw Cotter looking at me. From the deck he must have seen everything. But I ignored him too. I walked out to the parking lot, and when I was out of sight of the deck and the courts I broke into a jog, and when I hit Geddes Road I started running. Next to hitting, running's the best thing to do before a big match.

NiNETEEN Snuffy was posing on the sidewalk in front of the house. He lifted his head as I came up. I patted him. Snuff's not a very emotional dog, but he's loyal.

Matt's Cadillac was in the driveway. She must have called him the minute I left. It was a long time before dinner. I rattled the screen door latch a few times before I went in. Snuff came in behind me. Matt was sitting in the yellow wing chair, holding a newspaper. It was the chair Dad used to read the paper in too.

"Hey, there he is."

"Hello, Matt."

"Welcome home, Buddy Berger."

"Is Buddy back already?" Mom called.

148

"Yes."

She came into the living room. "Wasn't Chris there?"

"Uh . . . no."

"She's probably home then."

"I guess so."

Mom was puzzled. Why hadn't I stopped, then, at Chris's house, which was between our house and the club?

"I thought I'd take a shower," I said.

"Buddy, what's going on?" she asked.

I sat down on the couch near where Snuff had settled himself into another noble pose. He lifted his head to be scratched.

"She was there, wasn't she?"

I nodded.

"Was she with someone?"

I nodded again.

"Who?"

"Some guy."

"What guy?"

"A Swedish guy."

Mom looked relieved. "Oh, that's one of the Nielsen boys. They're a medical family that your father brought over. They're all tennis players. She was just being hospitable, Buddy."

"Really hospitable. She didn't have time to interrupt her game."

Matt laughed. "She's a tennis player all right. You got to get used to that in girls, kid. They're a strange species of human beings—female tennis players."

I flashed him a look, but it didn't register. He went right on.

"I got the same treatment myself a number of times," he said genially. "But I finally got her attention."

Mom blushed. She was both pleased and annoyed at Matt.

"You get on the phone and call her up, Buddy."

"No way."

"That's foolishness."

"I don't think so."

We faced each other. Her urging me to call Chris, me saying no. Again, the world turned upside down.

Matt said: "Why don't you make us a couple of tall lemonades, Helen?"

She looked at him. "All right."

Matt stretched his legs. For a moment he didn't say anything. We'd never really been alone before. I wondered what he was going to talk about. Give me advice about Chris, or talk about him and Mom?

"It's tough," he said. "Sometimes you're away a week it feels like a year."

God knows that was true.

"You had a bad week down there your Mom told me."

I nodded.

"She shouldn't have forced you to go down there. I told her that. But she can be pretty stubborn sometimes, can't she?"

"Yeah," I said.

He grinned. "I know that too. Well, she went to school a little on that one. And you paid for her lessons. Of course, there's another side to that coin."

"What's that?"

"With your being away . . . I guess I felt free to propose to your mom again. We had some long talks. They probably couldn't have happened if you'd been here."

He was right about that, I thought. I kept my eyes fixed on Snuffy as I scratched him.

"I guess she told you about us getting married this September?"

"Yeah."

150

I glanced at him. He was looking away too. We were both talking to each other and not looking at each other. How much more careful could two people get?

"I hope it's going to be OK with you, Buddy."

I looked at him. "It is, Matt."

He loooked at me hard to make sure . . . and then he relaxed, grinning. "Good. But I'd marry your mother even if you didn't approve, kid. I've been in love with her for seventeen years. Even before your father. But she wasn't in love with me. And your old man was pretty tough competition. Sports and brains and then medical school. But it goes to show you what patience will do. I hung in there. And here we are today. I'm a pretty happy guy, Buddy."

I nodded. I could understand it. But what was there for me to say? I'm glad you're happy, Matt? I hope you and my mom live happily ever after?

"I think the three of us are going to be OK together. We could make a pretty good team at that. I'm not your old man, but you and I can have some good times together, don't you think?"

"Sure."

"We can live on here or move down to my place on the river. You could have a sailboat down there. What do you think of that?"

"It'd be swell, Matt."

"Have you done much sailing, Buddy?"

I shook my head. "Maybe I can show you a few things. It's a great sport. Not the same kind of thing as tennis, but—"

"I'm through with tennis."

He grinned. "You had a bad week."

"It's more than that."

"A good night's sleep and a victory over your father, and you'll be the same old Buddy Berger. Terror of the courts."

No matter what happens tomorrow, I thought, I'd never

151

be the same old Buddy Berger. But I couldn't explain that to Matt. He was happy. He was going to be my stepfather. But he was the same old Matt. Nothing would ever change that. I envied him that.

The phone rang in the kitchen. I heard Mom put down the tray of lemonades to answer it.

"Hello, Dick. Yes, he's here. Of course. I'll get him."

She sounded relaxed on the phone with him.

"It's your father, Buddy."

"Can I . . . ?"

"Of course, take it upstairs."

She hung up as I got on the line.

"Hi," I said.

"Buddy, how did it go?"

"Fine."

"Chris just came in and told me she saw you out at the club."

That was his way of letting me know he knew what had happened.

"Yeah, I was out there for a little while."

"I asked Chris to introduce Eric Nielsen around. I think I told you about the Nielsens coming to town. His father's a surgeon from Stockholm who's going to be my right-hand man this year."

"Dad, it's no problem."

"As soon as I get off, I want to put Chris on. She wants to talk to you."

I bet she did.

"Dad, I'm telling you, everything's fine."

"Good. Now tell me about Tennis World. How was it?"

"It was fine."

"What's old Steger like on a day-to-day basis?"

"He's OK."

"You don't sound enthusiastic."

"No, it was OK. Really." Lies to Dad, truth to Mom. Another upside-down development. Or was I really talking to Chris through him?

"How about winter school?"

"I didn't make it."

"Good. I was hoping you wouldn't. What was it like? Lots of tennis?

"Yeah. Instruction in the mornings. Matches in the afternoon. Videotape at night."

"How'd you do in the matches."

"I won some, lost some."

"Can you come over and tell me about it?"

"I can't now. Matt's over here. . . ." I stopped. Should I tell Dad about Mom and Matt? I felt I should.

"Well, maybe later. I want to talk with you and hear all about it."

"Sure. Later."

"Tonight then?"

"I don't know, Dad."

I wanted badly to tell him about Matt and Mom. About Mom being so happy.

"Come over after supper."

"I don't think I can. You see, Mom and Matt . . . do you know?"

"What?"

"They're going to get married."

Dad was silent. He hadn't known.

"Mom's really happy. She's sorry she made me go to Tennis World. She's different."

"I think it's wonderful," Dad said quietly. "I'll call her later. Buddy, Chris is standing here. If I don't see you tonight, I'll see you tomorrow."

"Court One. Sampson Park. For all the marbles in town."

He laughed. "Whatever happens, it'll be fun, won't it, son?"

"Yes, Dad."

"Here's Chris."

"Buddy?"

"Yeah."

She waited. Giving my father time to leave.

I didn't say anything. If she wanted to fill silences, let *her*.

Finally she said: "What happened today?"

I cleared my throat. "What happened today was that I came home and went out to the courts first thing (that was a lie) to see you and you're hitting with some Swedish meatball and you don't even say hello."

"I did say hello and he's not a meatball."

"You didn't say hello and he is a meatball."

"Buddy, we were in the middle of *hitting*."

"So what? We hadn't seen each other for a week."

"Why didn't you write?"

"I started to, but I was having such a lousy time I didn't want to write about it."

"Eric says it's a good time down there."

"He *would* like it down there."

"They have lots of parties, he said."

"Yes, but I didn't go to them."

"I bet."

"Well, I didn't."

"So why didn't you write?"

"I didn't write because I had nothing to write about except how much I hated the place. Why didn't you write me?"

"*You* went away."

"Well, I'm not going away again."

"What about winter school?"

"I didn't make it."

"Why not?"

"Steger didn't like me."

"You, or how you play?"

"It's the same thing to him."

"I don't get it."

"He doesn't think I want to be a champ. He doesn't think I'm willing to make the sacrifices to be great."

"But you are."

"No, I'm not."

"But Buddy, you've got to be."

"Why?"

"Because you're good."

She sounded so much like my mother it was unreal.

"Can we talk about something else? Look, can I come over right now?"

Even as I said that, I remembered I'd told Dad I couldn't. Maybe Chris and I could meet halfway. It was suddenly very important to meet right away.

She hesitated. "Buddy, the Nielsens are downstairs. They're staying for supper."

"Oh."

"It's not what you think, Buddy. Eric's a neat guy. If you gave yourself a chance, you'd like him. He's been all around the world."

"Doesn't he know any girls his own age?"

"He's only seventeen."

"He looks more like seventy."

"Buddy, you're being very dumb and childish."

"Am I? What about you, Chris? I seem to remember something you said on the phone the night before I left. Do you remember?"

"You said it too."

"We both said it. And I guess it doesn't mean very much to you any more, does it?"

She was silent a moment. "I don't know," she said.

How could you be in love with someone one week and out of love the next? Could a big Swedish meatball do that to you?

"Well, I guess I don't know either any more. I hope you and Bjorn Borg, or whatever his name is, have a great time together. I hope he takes you down to Tennis World to some of the beer-drinking parties they have down there. I hope you and he—"

The phone clicked shut in my ear. I stood there listening to a loud, angry dial tone. And then I hung up too. My knees felt weak. Did things end like that? Why had I even said what I did? Oh, Chris. . . .

"Are you off the phone, Buddy?" Mom called up.

"Yes."

"Then come down and have your lemonade. It's practically all ice water now."

I went downstairs. They were sitting there, waiting for me, looking anxiously up at me.

"What did you and he talk about so long?" Mom asked.

I shook my head.

Matt asked: "Did you tell him about us, kid?"

I nodded.

"What did he say?"

"He was glad. He said he'd call Mom later and tell her himself."

Matt looked pleased. "Dick's all right. He was married to the wrong woman for too long a time, but he's all right. Now all we've got left to do is beat his pants off tomorrow."

Mom pretended to look shocked. " 'We,' Matt Bigby? Is Buddy doing it for *us* now?"

156

Matt turned all shades of red. Mom laughed at him. And then Matt laughed too.

My lemonade was all ice water. But I didn't mind. And I didn't really mind sitting there watching them in their happiness. It made me feel old and cynical. I wondered whether I should tell them Chris and I had just broken up; I decided not to. Let them find out for themselves tomorrow, when Chris showed up rooting for my father.

I finished the lemonade and went upstairs. They didn't even notice when I left.

TWENTY My story really ends here.

You've had enough tennis by now anyway. Enough backhands and forehands, drop shots and serves, Gatorade and polite applause from spectators.

Or maybe it's that I don't want to go into the details of how I lost to my father for the one-thousandth-and-one time. All I know is that I did not quit. I worked, I made him run, and he beat me. In a best-of-five-set final, he won the first set 6–3, the second set 7–5, and the third set 7–6 in a tie-breaker.

We had one rally that went on for about five minutes, it felt like. He had me on the defensive, driving me around the court, and then he came to the net. I didn't try to lob or moon-ball, but I drove one right at him as hard as I could. He barely got it back. I came in and drove to his forehand alley. He dove for it and half-volleyed it back over my head. I ran back and hit a forehand drive over my shoulder, deep to his backhand. He anticipated and drove a top-spin backhand to my forehand. And it started all over again. Good offense, good defense, hard running, hard shots, and then I missed the line by inches.

He stood there, leaning on his racket, puffing, sweating, and grinning. "Good point, Buddy," he called out.

I nodded. Everyone clapped. It was some of the best tennis of the tournament. The fact was I was coming closer and closer all the time. After the match someone yelled that I'd get him next year.

"No," I announced, "I'm all through with tennis. I'm quitting."

That got a big laugh because they thought I was joking. And Ann Lamson wrote it up for the *Arborville News*, saying: "After the match Buddy Berger jokingly announced his retirement at fifteen from tournament tennis." But I wasn't joking. And Dad knew it.

Because when we were alone and done with all the picture-taking and hand-shaking and the congratulating which included Mom congratulating him and telling me I had played a great match (this was just before she went out and demolished Mrs. Brady to win her umpteenth women's title), and Matt pumping my hand and then Dad's, and Dad, in turn, congratulating Matt on *his* "victory," and even Mom and Carol exchanging smiles—after all that and the trophy presentation by Paul Donaldson, Dad and I were alone in the parking lot by his car. And he said to me:

"You'll be back, Buddy. I know it and you know it. You're right to take a break now, but don't sell yourself short. This was the last time I'll ever beat you. We both know that. You're a fine tennis player, and you'll always be one. You've got tennis in your bloodstream. You were born and brought up on tennis. There's no way you won't play tennis all your life. Not for a living, maybe, but for life. Which is more important."

He talked so easily, so wisely, holding the big winner's trophy in his hand. I wasn't really interested though. I didn't

158

want to talk about tennis. I wanted to know how Chris was, had she said anything to him about me? She hadn't come to the match today. Carol had. Maybe I should have asked Carol.

Finally, I just blurted it out: "How is Chris?"

"She's all right, Buddy. You're both all right."

"I don't think so."

"Buddy," he said, and he let his big trophy rest on the hood of the Rambler (it was no problem for me to hold my runner-up's trophy), "you're both young. In some ways what happened this summer might have been a good thing. . . ." I stared at him. I was suddenly getting the feeling that maybe this Eric Nielsen business hadn't been all Chris's idea. He went on smoothly. "A few years from now you'll be going off to college . . . so will Chris. You'll be widening your horizons, meeting new people, having new experiences. That's important."

"But I love Chris, Dad. And she loves me."

He nodded. "I know how hard it is, Buddy. It's always hard. I know . . . . " He hesitated. "Buddy, I married my high-school sweetheart. I know what happens when you get too involved too early, when you don't move off and see the world on your own, make new friends. I know, Buddy . . . ."

For a second I couldn't look at him. It was so unfair. He wasn't me, I wasn't him. Chris wasn't Mom. Who gave him the right?

He put a hand on my shoulder. We were the same height. Next year I'd be bigger.

"Buddy, time's a greater healer. . . . You've got to believe that."

He said it like a doctor, and I think he believed it.

But I don't. I've learned a lot since that moment in the parking lot with Dad, standing there with our two gleaming

159

tennis trophies. I've learned that time is no healer at all. What time does is make hurts permanent so that they get covered up. Covered up so no one can see they're still there . . . except you.

I didn't see Chris the rest of the summer. July dragged into August, and I dragged with it. I got a job at the public library shelving books for two dollars an hour and swam at the city pool on Fuller Road. I didn't want to run into Chris at the club. Someone told me she had jumped three places on the junior ladder and was breathing hard on Janet Sklar's neck. I heard too that she and Eric Nielsen had won a mixed-doubles tournament at the club.

I didn't play much tennis. When I felt the need for exercise I'd hit against the backboard at Sampson, and if someone asked me to play with him, I would. Whether he was good or lousy. I didn't play in any tournaments.

Some of my friends bugged me—Cotter, Joel Cohen, Hannigan—but I told them I was laying off, so would they kindly lay off me. They took the hint.

Mom didn't bug me at all. She was busy with other things.

She and Matt got married the last week in September. They were married by Judge Lenaghan at City Hall, and Mrs. Brady and I were the witnesses. I guess I was the best man because I handed Matt the ring. It was a funny feeling.

Mom and Matt went on a honeymoon trip to the Caribbean, and I stayed alone in our house. The second night they were gone Dad called. School had begun, and I was reading a play by Shakespeare. Once you get into it and forget the funny language, or stop looking words up all the time, Shakespeare's plays are OK, but till you get inside them, they're rough going. I was glad when the phone interrupted.

"Buddy, what are you doing tonight?"

"Studying."

"How about taking a break and coming over for a while?"

I considered it for a split second. "No, thanks, Dad. I'm hitting the books pretty good." What a lie.

"When are they coming back, Buddy?"

"Sunday night."

"Who's cooking for you?"

"The whole town, it seems. I've been invited out practically every night this week, and Mom's left a full refrigerator too."

"How about coming over for dinner tomorrow night?"

"No, thanks, Dad. I'm really all booked up."

That wasn't quite the truth. I *had* been invited out for every night, but I hadn't accepted. The truth was I kind of liked being on my own. And anyway, I wasn't quite ready to go over there. I was doing pretty well on getting Chris out of my system. Going over there might just blow everything.

"I haven't seen you in a while, son. How about hitting some balls at the park tomorrow? I think I can get away early from the hospital."

"Dad, I'm really all through with tennis."

"I'm not talking about tennis."

"I know you're not, but I've got a lot of homework. I'm into Shakespeare, Pop. He's that dude who wrote all those cool plays."

I was trying to be funny. Dad wasn't amused. "You're sounding foolish, Buddy. Not like yourself. We would all like to see you."

"I appreciate that, but can I take a rain check for a while? Give Carol and Chris my best regards. I'll see you later, Dad."

I hung up quickly because I had tears in my eyes and didn't want Dad to hear them. It was just plain silly. I should be over that. It was his idea that Chris and I had been getting too involved. What did he want from me now? I wasn't a tennis ball to be pounded this way and that over some invisible net. No, I didn't need Dad or Carol or Chris or Mom or Matt or anyone. I had myself, and that was enough.

Myself and Snuffy, who lay at my feet, half-asleep.

It's hard to go on reading Shakespeare through wet eyes and a churning heart, so I tapped Snuffy on his rear end. "C'mon, old man, let's go for a walk."

We walked over to Sampson Park, which was empty except for the burn-outs who smoked around the warming shelter at night.

It was a beautiful, starry night and Snuffy and I walked alongside the dark tennis courts and up the little hill at the far end. Snuffy trotted about twenty feet ahead of me, investigating every tree and bush. Snuff thought after thirteeen years he owned the park and always sniffed and was miffed to find other dogs used his trees too. He restaked all his claims immediately.

I climbed the little hill and looked down on the world's oldest, weediest, most cracked public courts. A long way from Tennis World's glossy surfaces. But this was tennis too. People's tennis, but tennis.

Across the park, under the overhang of the shelter (which was only open during ice-skating time) I saw the glow of cigarettes. It reminded me of the party in Ellsworth Vines House. Kids cheating on the rules. I guess they had to do it to survive—all of them.

Everyone was busy surviving.

Mom was surviving. Chris was surviving. Down in Tennis World, where the lopsided kids took out their hate in banging tennis balls, Carmody and Norton had survived by being cynical. Out in California, Nancy Ross was probably surviving *her* tennis family.

And I had survived too. I had survived Tennis World; I had survived Mom; I would survive Chris.

But I wondered if I would ever love anyone again as I had loved Chris. And then I wondered if I'd ever loved her in the first place.

I mean: How could you really love anyone if you were always thinking about yourself? Chris said I thought too much, and she was right. She'd said it about my tennis game, and she was right there too. Love and tennis. I had failed at both.

So where did that leave me? What kind of person was I? What kind of person was I going to be?

Oh, leave your mind alone, Buddy Berger! Look at the stars.

I lay down on the hill and looked up. Snuffy, slowly and carefully, took a prone position at my feet. He looked at the park; I looked at the stars. There were millions and millions of them.

Somewhere in a distant galaxy there had to be a planet like ours where everything had fallen right. And maybe on that planet there was a small hill like this one and maybe a kid like me was lying on top of it, with his dog lying at his feet, looking at the stars too.

They probably didn't play tennis on that other planet. They probably played some kind of space game or science-fiction game. Only they didn't call it space or science fiction. They probably called it . . . tennis.

I laughed out loud. Snuffy's ears pricked. He looked at me inquiringly.

"You're absolutely right, old man. It's time to go home."

I got up, and Snuff struggled to his feet. He stretched his legs carefully and then trotted off down the hill. I came after him. We trotted home together.